I0687444

Landlocked

by

Marilyn Baron

This is a work of fiction. Names, characters, places, and incidents are either the product of the author's imagination or are used fictitiously, and any resemblance to actual persons living or dead, business establishments, events, or locales, is entirely coincidental.

Landlocked

COPYRIGHT © 2015 by Marilyn M. Baron

Contact Information: info@thewildrosepress.com

Cover Art by *Debbie Taylor*

The Wild Rose Press, Inc.
PO Box 708
Adams Basin, NY 14410-0708
Visit us at www.thewildrosepress.com

Publishing History
First Crimson Rose Edition, 2015
Print ISBN 978-1-5092-0296-6
Digital ISBN 978-1-5092-0297-3

Published in the United States of America

He was too freaking gorgeous with his chiseled movie-star face and a buff body to match. He extended his hand, and she stood up to shake it. But for a moment, he'd rendered her incoherent.

"Welcome to our little part of—"

"I've already had the 'little part of heaven,' speech from your receptionist," Amelia said when she rediscovered her voice.

Alec skewered her with a piercing look from his fathomless blue eyes.

"You think I'm a hillbilly." His deadpan delivery indicated it was more of a statement than a question.

"You must be a mind reader."

"Don't have to be. It's written all over your face."

"Okay, I have to ask. What's a Duke grad doing in a backwater town like Confrontation? And I use the term *town* loosely."

"Practicing law," Alec answered dryly.

"I've already contacted a local broker/realtor named Barry Brady, and he referred me to you. He said he'd looked at the papers I faxed over and that we couldn't proceed with the sale. That's when he recommended I see you. Your secretary's named Brady, too. Is everyone in this town related?"

Alec's face flashed a barely disguised smile. Must be an inside joke.

"Pretty much, ma'am."

"I'm glad I could amuse you. Do you all intermarry up here in Confrontation?"

"I'm not married."

"No cousins available?"

"Is that a serious question?"

Praise for Marilyn Baron

"Baron offers a bit of everything…. There's humor, infidelity, murder, mayhem, and a neatly drawn conclusion."

~RT Book Reviews (4.5 Stars)

UNDER THE MOON GATE: "A surefire blockbuster… a treasure trove of mystery and intrigue. It sparkles with romance."

~Andrew Kirby

"Historical romance at its best."

~TripFiction

"A great job of bringing Bermuda during the WWII era to life."

~PJ Ausdenmore, The Romance Dish

"An enjoyable read from start to finish…family, friends, enemies, intrigue and suspense."

~Romance Junkies (4 Blue Ribbons)

SIXTH SENSE: "A great mix of romance, spinetingling suspense, and real hope for two jaded individuals."

~Tami Brothers

"An intriguing, albeit reluctant, psychic detective."

~Pauline Michael, Night Owl Romance (3 Stars)

"*KILLER CRUISE*: "An entertaining mystery….Not everything…is what it seems."

~Delane, Coffee Time Romance & More (4 Cups)

THE WIDOWS' GALLERY: "I enjoyed the romantic fantasy and learned why many readers are attracted to this genre of entertaining literature. I also appreciated Marilyn Baron's ability to hook the reader's interest and keep the action moving at a fast pace. Any art lover will enjoy this novel."

~Dub Taft

Dedication

This book is dedicated to my father, George Meyers, a product of the Great Depression, who loved the concept of owning land. He owned and sold properties in Vero Beach, FL, and Arden, NC, and a cabin and acreage in rural western NC.

All of our vacations growing up centered around visiting these properties. After his death, when we tried to sell his mountaintop property, we discovered it was landlocked, and therefore unsalable. The whole tangled process was laughable, and that's how *Landlocked* was conceived. My father had always envisioned that he'd build a vacation home on his property for all his children and their children to visit. Although that never happened, I did get a book out of the experience.

Hope you have plenty of land in Heaven, Dad.

Marilyn Baron's Contest Wins

The Colonoscopy Club (now the published novel *STONES*) finaled in the GRW Unpublished Maggie Awards for Excellence in 2005 in the Single Title category.

~*~

The Edger won first place in the Suspense Romance category of the 2010 Ignite the Flame Contest, sponsored by the Central Ohio Fiction Writers chapter of RWA.

~*~

Sixth Sense won the GRW 2012 Unpublished Maggie Award for Excellence in the Paranormal/Fantasy Romance category.

~*~

Significant Others was a finalist in the 2014 GRW Published Maggie Awards for Excellence in the Novel With Strong Romantic Elements category.

Part I

A Cabin in the Mountains

Marilyn Baron

Chapter One

"You're selling Grandpa's land?"

Amelia Rushing gaped at her grandmother, who was seated gracefully on a flowered gold brocade couch, comfortably cocooned in her retirement condo in South Florida, her cane resting carelessly against the arm of the couch.

Katherine Rushing planted her hands on either side of her hips and thrust her head up stubbornly. "It's my land, now, Amelia."

"But you and Grandpa bought that property forty years ago. Grandpa wanted to build a house where all his children and grandchildren could go for family vacations."

Katherine shook her head. "That was his vision, not mine, but we haven't been back there in thirty years, and I need the money now. Your father is talking about moving me into one of those old-age homes, and how am I going to pay for that?"

"It's an independent living facility, Grandma."

"Don't sugarcoat it, Amelia. It's where old people go to die. My friend Phyllis calls it Heaven's Waiting Room."

"Grandma!"

"Your dad thinks I have dementia."

"You're just a little forgetful. That's natural for a woman of your age."

Katherine looked directly into her granddaughter's eyes. "You mean for an old woman. We both know it's more than that. He and your mother took me on an outing the other day and somehow we ended up at Eternal Gardens. The place looks like a funeral home. It will probably be my final resting place. Most of those people don't know what's going on around them. We had lunch there, and your parents were raving about how beautiful the place was and all the activities there were and how they'd like to move there and get two chef-prepared meals a day and an option for lunch. I'd like to see your mother live in that place. The next thing I knew, your father had signed me up. He's moving me in next month."

"Did you agree to that?"

"What choice do I have? Your father thinks it's the best thing for everyone." Katherine mumbled something under her breath that sounded like, "They want to wash their hands of me."

"It's a studio apartment," Katherine said. "When we were walking around the unit your dad picked out, I said, 'Now I'm in my living room.' Then I moved forward a few steps and said, 'Now I'm in my bedroom.' Then I walked a few feet over and I told him, 'Now I'm standing in my kitchen.' At least the bathroom has a separate door.

"So I don't really need to be worrying about that land. Besides, everyone in our family lives in Florida, and the land is on a mountaintop in rural North Carolina. Owning it doesn't make any sense."

Amelia pursed her lips. She could hardly argue with her grandmother's reasoning. "But Dad says he and his sisters used to love the family trips to the cabin

4

when he was growing up."

"Yes, and he hasn't been back since," countered Katherine, fingering her cane, lost in her memories. "None of your aunts have expressed an interest in the property, either. It was your grandfather's dream. We did love it up there. It was so quiet and peaceful, far away from the real world, like Shangri-La. There was even mist on the mountains. Those mountains are some of the oldest in the world, and they go all the way up to heaven. Grandpa used to sit on the front porch in his rocker, and I used to mosey. He loved to go ruby mining, and sometimes we'd both go traversing the property, with walking sticks he made from tree branches. Land was so important to your grandfather. He grew up in the Great Depression, you know."

How many times had Amelia heard her grandfather's story of deprivation?

"He was convinced there were rubies on his property," Katherine said. "Later, the dream of building a nice vacation home all the grandchildren could enjoy is what kept him going. But now he's gone, and because of my arthritis I can't really travel, so I won't be going up there anymore. I want to sell the land before I completely lose my mind."

"Don't say that."

"That's what happens when you get to be my age. I'm not completely gone yet, but I want to tie up loose ends while I still have something going on upstairs, and I don't mean here on the fourth floor. I don't want to saddle my children with the burden of selling this property or have them squabbling over the land. I want this handled so I can go in peace."

"Go where?"

5

"You know, wherever it is people go after they leave this earth."

"Grandma, I wish you would stop talking like that."

"Why? Does it make you uncomfortable? How do you think it makes me feel? Would you like a piece of key lime pie, dear? Mrs. Bailey from next door brought it over this morning."

Amelia had already eaten a delicious slice of Mrs. Bailey's key lime pie with a generous helping of whipped cream when she arrived at her grandmother's condo, but she didn't want to call attention to the fact that her grandmother had already forgotten.

"I'd love a slice, Grandma. Let me get us each a serving."

"I love key lime pie. Did I tell you Mrs. Bailey made it fresh this morning? You know, there are no key limes on our property in North Carolina."

Her father had told Amelia that his mother was repeating herself more frequently, and she had tossed it off as the normal forgetfulness that comes with old age. But now that she witnessed the behavior in person, the signs seemed more ominous.

Amelia looked across the room at a painting of a cabin in the woods. She'd never seen the property for herself, but Katherine said that was a picture of their cabin in the mountains. The painting had always been her favorite of her grandmother's possessions. It was a Moss Hathaway, one of the last paintings he'd done before he disappeared thirty years ago. It was probably worth a small fortune, but her grandparents had never considered selling it. And when she asked where her grandmother had found the painting, she refused to say.

"I want you to have that painting when I'm gone," Katherine stated now. "I know how much you love it. And you're the only one in the family who can appreciate it, with your degree in art history. But I don't want you to sell it."

Amelia stared at the painting. "Thank you, Grandma. It will always remind me of you and Grandpa."

Amelia walked to the kitchen and cut two more slices of key lime pie and placed them on the dessert plates they'd already used. At this rate, she was going to turn into a blimp. It was a good thing she had canceled the wedding. She didn't need to fit into her wedding dress, so she could eat key lime pie to her heart's content. On her way back to the living room, she walked past the sliding glass door at the back of the condo and examined the darkening sky. She drew a sharp breath. The black clouds were a certain sign of a gathering storm.

Her cell phone beeped. It was an alert signaling bad weather in the area. Confirmation.

"I need to go," she announced abruptly, placing the plates on the coffee table in front of her grandmother.

"But you just got here."

"Grandma, actually I've been here for a while. Did you see the sky? The meteorologist on the news this morning mentioned some kind of system coming in from the Gulf. A stalled front, and they're predicting a bad rain storm. I just got a storm alert on my cell phone." Amelia paced the length of the condo and rechecked the sky from the front window.

"You must be channeling your grandfather. You've inherited his weather issues. What do you think will happen to you? It's just a little rain. It always rains in South Florida. You won't melt. You're weather-obsessed just like he was."

"Grandpa was a smart man. He'd understand I don't want to be out on the road in a thunderstorm," Amelia explained, taking another bite of pie. "There's so much traffic on the expressway. The car could skid, and I could get into a head-on collision, like that accident in Kendall yesterday where the woman was killed. And there's a hurricane forming over the Atlantic."

Amelia's heartthrobs were not movie actors or rock stars. They were meteorologists on The Weather Channel. Or storm chasers. In fact, she'd had an erotic dream last night about the sexy new weatherman on Channel 9, Gil Pomerance. During hurricane season she remained glued to the TV set and refused to travel on a plane to any destination from June to November.

"It's heading for Bermuda. It's nowhere near us," Katherine pointed out.

"Hurricanes are unpredictable. They can turn."

Katherine sighed. "Come sit with me, sweetheart. There's something I want to ask you."

Amelia's breath came out in rapid spurts. She pinched her hands until they hurt. Her grandmother had eaten her second slice of pie, so she cleared both plates from the table and put them in the sink. Then she sat down on the couch next to her grandmother and tried to settle her galloping heart.

"I've made up my mind. I want to sell the land."

"What does Dad say?"

"He says I should have sold it years ago, right after Grandpa died."

Amelia's grandmother got that faraway look whenever she talked about her husband of almost sixty years, twice as long as Amelia had been alive. What must it be like to have loved somebody for that long? In comparison, Amelia's relationships fizzled out in a matter of months. The concept of a long-lasting relationship was inconceivable to her. She was a loser in the love department. Not so long ago she thought she'd found Mr. Right. In fact, they were engaged, but she had called the wedding off last month. She and What's-His-Name had been sitting at the bar at a Miami restaurant when the server, built like a blonde Uber Barbie, came up and bent down right in front of her fiancé as she set a rare burger and fries on a plate before him. Barbie had been wearing what looked like a powder blue lace bra under a tight, clingy shirt, and everything she had to offer, and more, was sticking out. What's-His-Name didn't even pretend not to stare, open-mouthed, with his tongue hanging out.

Amelia couldn't believe how much he was salivating. It looked like he wanted to reach out and touch her. Or scarf her up for lunch as his second course, after the hamburger.

"Hello, I'm right here," Amelia had pointed out, like a harping fishwife.

What's-His-Name didn't take his eyes off the waitress but said, "What's wrong with looking? We're not married yet. I wouldn't be normal if I didn't look."

"It seems like you want to do a lot more than look."

"So what if I do?"

"I don't believe you just said that."

What's-His-Name took a bite of his burger, and

juice dripped down his chin. He just kept eating until he finished the entire burger and fries, like nothing was wrong. Amelia couldn't eat her seafood salad. She was waiting in vain for an apology or an admission or something. He didn't even notice she hadn't taken a bite of her meal.

The server came back, and when she brought the check she scribbled her phone number and the words "Call Me" on the customer receipt. Then she branded the receipt with her bright red lipstick. What's-His-Name, normally cheap, slapped a fifty down on the counter and then slipped the receipt into his pocket. Amelia reached into his pocket and pulled it out. The server was a skank, but What's-His-Name didn't have to pocket her telephone number.

What's-His-Name tried to grab the receipt out of her hand.

"You're not seriously going to call her, are you?"

"You know the rules, babe. Until there's a ring on my finger, I have the freedom to do whatever and whoever I want. I may as well get it out of my system before you tie the noose around my neck."

Amelia cleared her throat and overcame the urge to break the china plate over his head, burger juice and all. "That's *whom*ever I want, and I wasn't aware you felt so trapped." Amelia handed the crumpled receipt to What's-His-Name along with her engagement ring. "If that's the way you feel, by all means go ahead, get it out of your system."

"What are you doing?" he demanded.

"Setting you free so you can boink Burger Barbie's brains out."

What's-His-Name stared at the engagement ring in

his hand in disbelief. "What just happened? Why are you so pissed?"

"You were practically undressing that waitress right in front of me. That's not proper behavior for an engaged man. The only boobs you should be staring at or thinking about are mine."

What's-His-Name looked at her chest and then let his eyes roam back to the rack on Burger Barbie as if to say, *No contest. Who could blame me?*

"What do you think I did at my bachelor party in Vegas?"

"I don't know. What *did* you do?"

"Let off a little steam, like any normal guy."

Amelia frowned. "And by steam, do you mean that you actually slept with another woman?"

"What do you think goes on at those weekends?"

Amelia picked up her purse from the stool next to hers, slung it over her shoulder, and started to walk away.

What's-His-Name jerked her by the hand, pulling her back, and asked angrily, "You're not seriously calling off the wedding, are you?"

Amelia plucked his hand away from her arm. "What did you think would happen? You're obviously not ready to get married if you're ogling other women."

She walked away and never looked back. She erased What's-His-Name's memory from the database in her head and from her heart. There had to be someone else out there who wasn't such a colossal jerk, but she had little hope of finding the right someone.

"Amelia, why don't you slice us some of that key lime pie Mrs. Bailey brought over this morning? It's fresh."

"Grandma, we already had—" Amelia stopped herself and went back to slice the third piece of key lime pie, put it on a plate, and brought it in to her grandmother.

"Aren't you going to have a piece of pie? It looks delicious."

"I had a big breakfast."

Amelia glanced again at the picture of the cabin on the wall, and she had a sudden memory of her grandfather sitting in his chair at the kitchen table.

"Every time Dad came over, Grandpa would pull out his parcel maps and the Plat of Survey and regale him with stories about the North Carolina land. And now you want to sell it? That was Grandpa's legacy."

Katherine covered her granddaughter's hand with her own. "I'm just paying exorbitant insurance and taxes on property I haven't seen in thirty years. You all love the idea of the land, but you've never set foot on it."

"I wonder what it's worth?" Amelia asked, her brain kicking into realtor overdrive as she removed her grandmother's empty plate and put it with the other dishes in the sink.

"According to the tax people, it's worth a lot, or at least I'm paying taxes on a high property value. Anyway, your parents are too busy to handle this. You're a realtor, and I want you to sell the land."

Amelia hesitated. "Grandma, you know I just got my real estate license, and I don't have authority to sell real estate in North Carolina. You should get someone more experienced."

"You've got to start somewhere. It might as well be in North Carolina. And I know you need the money.

There will be a nice commission in it for you."

"Grandma, I don't want your money."

"You're my granddaughter. I know the sale would mean more to you than to some stranger in North Carolina. I'd like you to see firsthand what made your grandfather so happy. You will get the best price for me. If you have to hire an out-of-state lawyer, then go right ahead. Spend whatever you need. To tell you the truth, this land has been like an albatross around my neck. I encouraged your grandfather to sell it for years, but he refused. And I didn't have the heart or the will to tell him he'd made a mistake."

To Grandpa, purchasing the land had not been a mistake. He'd enjoyed the cabin during the years he and Grandma had actually vacationed there, and even after they stopped going to North Carolina he had been content to sit around the condo looking at maps of his property, reading the local newspaper from the community where the land was located, and gazing at the painting of the cabin in their condo. In his mind, it was comforting somehow to own the land. To imagine the possibilities. To dream his pipe dreams. But in reality the land was not doing anybody any good.

"Okay, I'll try to sell it for you," Amelia agreed. "Can you show me exactly what kind of property we're talking about?"

"Everything's in this cardboard box here on the coffee table."

"Grandma, you're not supposed to lift heavy boxes."

"I'm not completely incapacitated."

Amelia pulled the box toward her. She looked at her watch.

13

"But I need to leave by one o'clock to get a jump on the storm. I don't have to go all the way to North Carolina to sell the property, you know. I could hire a lawyer to handle the transaction."

"But I want you to go. If you're going to do something, then do it right, I always say. Anyway, I know you and What's-His-Name just broke up. Don't you have something better to do with your time than mope around?"

"What's-His-Name was a jerk," Amelia admitted. A jerk she had once thought might be The One. The problem was that Bimbo Barbie thought he might be The One for her, too. Her friends had confirmed the jerk and the bimbo had hooked up and continued to see each other. She could cross that restaurant off her list.

"I'm sorry to hear that. The right one will come along. There's always another train pulling into the station."

Amelia smiled. No one's train was interested in pulling into her station at the moment. In fact, the illusive train was rusting on the tracks.

"Maybe you'll find him where you least expect it. Maybe he's in North Carolina."

Amelia chuckled. "Grandma, that land is in hillbilly country. There's no one there I'd be interested in meeting."

"They don't have much use for us, either. They call us the Florida people. I remember the family who lived next door to our cabin, the Bradys, on Brady Cove Road. They had nine children. Each child's name began with a B. There was Betty Brady and Ben Brady, and their kids Bundy Brady, Bradley Brady, Butch Brady, Bunnie Brady, Buster Brady, Ben. Jr., and Betty's late-in-life triplets—Brenna, Barbara, and Bernice—Necey, they used to call her. Necey's son is a lawyer up there. You might start with him. And don't be so quick to judge people you don't know. Anyway, what do you have to stick around for?"

"My job."

"And how many sales have you made in the last three months?"

Amelia bit her bottom lip. "Well, none, yet."

"Then this will be your first."

"Are you just selling the land because you feel sorry for me and you want me to get a commission?"

"Of course not. I have complete confidence in you."

"I wish my parents did."

"Your parents love you."

"Maybe, but they don't think I can hold onto a successful career—or a man, even if the man was a scumbag."

"Nonsense."

"Let's face it. They thought I was crazy to major in art history, and maybe they were right. I couldn't find a job in my field. I'm not sure being a realtor is going to work out, either."

"Have a little faith in yourself," said Katherine, lifting a photo album from the pile. The sky began to rumble, and the lights in the living room flickered.

"Did you see that flash?" Amelia asked, rising suddenly. A few seconds later a thunderbolt shook the room. "Do you hear that? That was close." Amelia wrestled with her knuckles until they turned white.

"Amelia Analise Rushing. Sit down. You can wait for the storm to pass. Your grandfather's whole life is in this box." Katherine wiped a tear from her cheek. "Let's go through the box, and after we have a piece of that nice pie Mrs. Bailey from next door brought over—Did I tell you she made it fresh this morning?—you can stay awhile and I'll tell you a little bit about the neighbors and the town so you can get acclimated before you get to Confrontation."

Chapter Two

"There are actually two tracts of land," Katherine explained, pulling out the deeds and reading the descriptions. "The two parcels are situated in Bearmeat Brand in Confrontation Township, Jasper County, North Carolina.

"Tract One is more particularly described from the referenced deed BEGINNING on a Sourwood on the Graveyard Ridge, witnessed by a Maple and a Sourwood, at a corner of Glenn Nations and Paul Riverbrooks," Katherine continued. "Then in a northwesterly direction to a Poplar on the bank of Nancy Green Branch; thence in a northerly direction with a wire fence and the meanders of the ridge, approximately 935 feet to a Hickory in the line of said tract; then in a westerly direction with the line to a Sourwood at a corner of Taylor Parris and Paul Riverbrooks; then in a southerly direction with Madison Franklin's conditional line to a Spanish Oak; then with said conditional line to a Buckeye (corner of R. L. D. Standard); then in an easterly direction to a Hickory at a corner of Paul Riverbrooks; then up the ridge as it meanders approximately 400 feet to the point of BEGINNING, containing approximately twenty acres."

"That's insane," Amelia said.

"I'm reading right from the deed. That's exactly how the property is described. The land value of the first property is $93,300," Katherine read.

"Tract Two is more particularly described from the referenced deed BEGINNING on a stake near the top of the ridge west of the Bearmeat Branch on the north side of Jasper Creek, being a corner in John Harris's line," Katherine continued. "John Harris was a widower married to the former Gillian Billings. Then in a westerly direction with John Harris's line to the A. K. York corner in said line; then northwesterly with the A. K. York line to where it corners with Dan York and Glenn Nations; then in a northwesterly direction with the ridge up from the Mason Knob as it meanders to B.C. Lofting's line; then in a southerly direction with the Lofting line to the point of BEGINNING, containing forty acres more or less. The land value of the second tract is $267,000."

"That's some serious money," Amelia said. "But what does the fact that John Harris is a widower have to do with anything?"

"Every name and place is important. These were real people. It helped people identify the property."

"How am I ever going to find that property? How will I know which sourwood tree to start from? And what's a sourwood tree, anyway?"

"That's why you're going to need the help of one of the locals, maybe that Brady boy."

"Billy Bob Brady?"

"I don't know his name, but I'll look it up for you. It's in his mother's last letter to me."

Amelia rolled her eyes. "I guess I ought to pay the Clampetts a visit."

"It's the Bradys, dear."

"More like the Brady bunch. I'll bet they don't

have a complete brain between them."

"That's just a stereotype. They don't think much of us, either. They call us the Florida people." Katherine cleared her throat and pulled out some oversized sheets of paper. "Grandpa paid good money to obtain a survey on both pieces of land not long before he left us. These ought to help. And the cold spring that serves the city originates on our land."

"You mean your land is the water source for the township?"

"That's right. It's a working spring that has a continuous flow of water."

"What about the cabin?"

"Well, for a while we were renting it out to Betty's youngest, Necey. She was paying rent, not much, but then the checks stopped coming."

"Do you think the family is still living in your cabin?"

"I have no idea."

"Probably squatters."

"We're not using it, so—"

"Grandpa wasn't much of a businessman, was he?" Amelia observed. What had possessed her grandfather to buy property on an isolated mountaintop?

"Your grandfather was a good man."

"Sorry," Amelia relented. "I know he was."

"How soon can you leave?"

Amelia contemplated her less-than-busy schedule. She didn't even have any listings. Considering her lease had just run out, she was currently living with her parents, was just about flat broke and owed thousands of dollars on her college loan, and What's-His-Name had made it clear that he preferred the company of an overendowed cocktail waitress (who probably didn't have a deathly fear of inclement weather), there was no legitimate reason she couldn't get into her car and head north immediately.

No reason except that the sky was getting darker by the minute, and that meant heavy rain, which inevitably meant lightning. Florida was the lightning capital of the U.S. And North Carolina was also one of the states that had the most lightning deaths and injuries every year. Amelia was well aware of the facts: that lightning is the most dangerous and frequently encountered weather hazard people experience each year; that there are approximately 100,000 storms in the U.S. each year; and that lightning is the number-one cause of storm-related deaths. Those statistics were emblazoned in her memory, and they were handy statistics to have, say, at cocktail parties when the conversation began to flag.

From the window, Amelia saw an ominous-looking funnel-like cloud drop from the mother ship. Was that a tornado forming? If it was a tornado, it could touch down at any moment. And she couldn't—wouldn't—drive in the rain. She'd have to check the weather forecast before she left Miami.

Amelia sprang to her feet. "Grandma, I need to leave *now*."

"But you were going to stay for lunch."

"Gotta go."

Amelia shivered, expecting the familiar onset of a full-blown panic attack. The breath caught in her throat. Her heartbeat was out of sync. Gulping, she tried unsuccessfully to inhale a calming breath. She felt like she was going to collapse. Breathing into a paper bag might help, but she didn't want to alarm her grandmother. Normal people could not understand her visceral reaction to rain. It wasn't just rain but all the bad things that went with it. Thunder, lightning, tornadoes, and hail. The sense of dread and foreboding, the fear of driving with no visibility on the turnpike or the expressway, of being immobilized by the hypnotic rhythm of the windshield wipers in a blinding storm. Worrying about whether the car in front of her had its lights on and whether she was going to crash into it or get struck by lightning or go careening off the edge of an overpass.

She had often envisioned her car a heap of metal wrapped around a tree. Or at the bottom of a lake or canal. And she would be struggling in vain to get out of the car, up to the surface. How many tragic stories had she read in the newspaper or seen on TV? It could happen at any time, to anyone. It just hadn't happened to her, yet.

Miami was on the cusp of hurricane season. Summer was the season of dangerous storms and tremendous floods. Amelia was very sensitive to thunder. When she knew a storm was coming and she was at home, she'd put her car in the garage, unplug all the appliances, and sit in a chair away from the window, huddled up under a blanket, to protect herself from flying glass, until the storm passed. There weren't any basements in Florida, so she'd take refuge sometimes in her closet, if it was a really bad storm. And she made up any excuse to avoid driving in extreme weather. That set the tone for a slim social life, because it rained almost every day in Miami.

Amelia checked her iPhone. Tomorrow's forecast called for a sunny day up and down the East Coast. So she could start out at first light in the morning and make it all the way to Atlanta. No need to outrun the weather. She couldn't drive the sixteen straight hours to the cabin. The last thing she needed was to arrive in a godforsaken town, if Confrontation could even be called a town, in the boondocks of North Carolina, in the middle of the night. And her car wasn't exactly reliable. Plus she had a horrible sense of direction and she couldn't afford a GPS. It would be easier to find her way in daylight.

"Take plenty of pictures of the property," called Katherine, as Amelia hoisted the box of documents and hurried out of the condo before all hell broke loose and the bottom dropped out of the sky.

Chapter Three

Amelia scanned the law office of Alec Brady, surprised to see a framed diploma from Duke University School of Law on the wall.

"Welcome in," greeted the young receptionist.

Welcome in? What kind of a greeting was that? Some kind of strange North Carolina dialect?

"I had the worst time finding this place," Amelia complained.

"That's because Confrontation ain't even on the map," answered the receptionist, which explained why Amelia had despaired of ever finding it. It must be something like Walton's Mountain.

The receptionist told her to wait in "Billy Bob's" office until he returned from lunch. Not an auspicious beginning. Amelia's eyes were beginning to droop, her energy flagging after the long drive from Florida yesterday and the drive from Atlanta this morning. She was hungry, but she'd devoured all of her snacks. Admittedly, the scenery had been beautiful once she crossed the North Carolina state line, but she was tired of searching the sky for raindrops, her mood was crappy—and this jerk had the nerve to keep her waiting? When they had an appointment? Time obviously meant nothing to these mountain people.

Amelia pulled up her pantyhose and noticed a jagged run. Great. She'd snagged the stockings on

Bozo's scarred wooden desk. Dammit. She'd paid good money for these stockings. And money didn't grow on trees. Ordinarily, she wouldn't be caught dead in pantyhose, but she'd wanted to make a good impression. She pulled her dress down past her knees to cover the hole. Who'd invented pantyhose, anyway? No wonder they were the weapon of choice for serial killers.

And speaking of weapons, she fingered the loaded Smith & Wesson Chief's Special .40 in her handbag. You couldn't be too careful with all the psychos out there kidnapping and killing realtors. Her company had started arming its agents for their own protection. Along with her real estate license, she now had a license to carry. Confrontation struck Amelia as just the type of lawless place where she'd need a gun. She probably should have learned how to handle the firearm before she struck out for no-man's land. But too late now. She was here. And the sooner she concluded her business, the better. She was going to make this sale or die trying.

The office door opened and suddenly her image of a small-town, redneck lawyer flew out the window. This couldn't possibly be Billy Bob. He was too freaking gorgeous, with his chiseled movie-star face and a buff body to match. He extended his hand, and she stood up to shake it. But for a moment, he'd rendered her incoherent.

"Welcome to our little part of—"

"I've already had the 'little part of heaven,' speech from your receptionist," Amelia said when she rediscovered her voice.

Alec skewered her with a piercing look from his

fathomless blue eyes.

"You think I'm a hillbilly." His deadpan delivery indicated it was more of a statement than a question.

"You must be a mind reader."

"Don't have to be. It's written all over your face."

"Okay, I have to ask. What's a Duke grad doing in a backwater town like Confrontation? And I use the term *town* loosely."

"Practicing law," Alec answered dryly.

"I've already contacted a local broker/realtor named Barry Brady, and he referred me to you. He said he'd looked at the papers I faxed over and that we couldn't proceed with the sale. That's when he recommended I see you. Your secretary's named Brady, too. Is everyone in this town related?"

Alec's face flashed a barely disguised smile. Must be an inside joke.

"Pretty much, ma'am."

"I'm glad I could amuse you. Do you all intermarry up here in Confrontation?"

"I'm not married."

"No cousins available?"

"Is that a serious question?"

"You know you're allowed to marry your first cousin in North Carolina."

"I'll bet you think that's funny."

Amelia suppressed a smile. Then she plastered on her serious getting-down-to-business face. "Let's get down to business." Dorky. She'd never used that expression before. But Billy Bob was making her nervous. She couldn't look away from him. Hopefully, he didn't notice.

"Ma'am, I've looked over the documents my

cousin faxed me yesterday. I've done some preliminary research. You said over the phone you wanted to sell the property. My cousin is right. There's a slight problem."

"What kind of problem is that? And why are you calling me 'ma'am'? I'm not your mother."

The light went out in the man's eyes at the mention of his mother. "It's a sign of respect around these parts." He didn't just say *around these parts*, did he?

The lawyer continued, "In researching the property, I discovered that the county mapping system plat is not accurate and this property is landlocked. Any buyer you do get will back out. You don't have an easement from any of the surrounding landowners. You can't sell without an easement. You can't even step foot on the property yourself without an easement. Therefore, that land has no value to you. And I'd advise any client coming to me about purchasing this land to walk away—no, to run away—from a deal like that. It's not worth tangling with all the disputes that will likely arise."

"Is this some kind of a bad joke?"

"It's the law, Miss Rushing. You don't have access. Your property is landlocked."

"What exactly does that mean?"

"It means you have no access or egress to a public road and your property cannot be reached except by crossing another person's property."

Amelia tapped her finger on the Property Plat impatiently. "Look right here. It appears there is access to the property on Soil Road, and here's another road that gives us access in the northeast corner of the property. That's a road around my property."

Alec placed his finger beside hers on the plat and triggered an electric jolt when they came into contact. "You are correct about the Soil Road reference. And it does look like the property has multiple points of access, but there are no roads into or out of your tract. The problem is that Sparks Road is south of the property and you would have to go through the Brady property in order to get to Soil Road. I don't see any reference of that easement mentioned in the deed. The only road up the mountain and down is owned by my family, and legally you can't access it. Soil Road is a misnomer. It's simply a description of a dirt clearing "road" that can barely be seen in the aerial view. If someone wants your tract, they would have to build a road right through one of the other owners' property. But there is no true adjacent road that could be used to egress from the property. The best proposal I can think of is to try to sell your tracts to the owners of the adjacent land who are already on a county road."

"Those owners being your family. And I assume you'll advise me to sell at a substantial loss?"

"For whatever you can get. My cousin's assessment was that both of your tracts are on very steep mountainside with limited flat areas for building."

"But the properties have great mountain views."

Alec shook his head. "Every piece of property around here has great mountain views. We're in the mountains. You're being unrealistic, Miss Rushing."

"Are you trying to outslick me, Slick? With your ma'ams and Miss Rushings?"

"Maybe I'm trying to disarm you."

"What you're doing is jerking me around. I don't have access to my own property? Then why has my grandmother been paying taxes all these years—at an exorbitant rate, I might add? I did the research. The surrounding properties are taxed at half the rate she pays. Do Florida people pay a different rate of tax than the natives?"

"It's not supposed to work like that."

"Why don't you tell me how it's supposed to work in Bradyville?"

"The town's called Confrontation."

"Then I'll call the police."

"Don't expect any support from the police, the town, or the county in a right-of-way dispute."

"What if I sue?"

"My family will gate the path so you can't drive a car onto the property."

"What happened to the concept of being a good neighbor?"

"We don't recognize that concept with outsiders."

"I'm hardly an outsider. My family has owned this land for forty years, and I need to get on that property. My grandmother wants me to take some pictures of the cabin and the land for sentimental reasons. I came here to sell the property, and I'm not leaving until I do."

"Uh, that might not be possible."

"How so?"

"I'm living in the cabin."

"You're living in *my* cabin?"

"Temporarily."

"How long have you been living there?"

Alec cleared his throat. "Three years."

"Three years? You call that temporary? And why would you want to live in a dilapidated cabin, anyway?"

"First of all, it's not dilapidated. I've fixed it up over the years. It's pretty livable, with the improvements I've made."

"Can't you afford a place of your own?"

"My mother is…" Alec hesitated. "Was sick. She was dying. Um, she's gone now. I was offered a job at a big law firm in New York when I graduated, but I decided to come home and take care of my mother. She needed me. I like being near family. My family depends on me."

"That's admirable," Amelia admitted. "So you both lived in the cabin?"

"It was convenient. Right next door to her two sisters. Before that, my cousin lived there, but she let my mother have it."

"Your cousin let your mother have my cabin? Let me guess. Your cousin's last name is Brady."

"Well, yes."

Amelia's eyes widened. "This is unbelievable. I feel like I'm in an episode of *The Beverly Hillbillies*. That's my grandmother's cabin, and no one has paid her rent for thirty years."

Alec's face reddened. "Are you always this condescending?"

"I might be considered condescending if what I said weren't true. Your cousin was squatting. Your mother was squatting, and you are squatting."

"We just figured that—"

"You just figured that you'd take advantage of an elderly woman you knew could not make it up here, and your cousin and your mother thought they'd live there rent-free."

"Haven't you ever heard of squatter's rights? It's

29

called adverse possession in North Carolina. We have legal title to the property because my family has continuously occupied the land for thirty years."

"You're making this up."

"I am not. It's a legal term. Are you a lawyer, Miss Rushing?"

Amelia frowned, opened her laptop and starting typing. Minutes later, her eyes brightened. "What about the concept of an easement implied by necessity?"

"Those don't just magically appear. There are a number of factors to be considered. First, there must be continued and uninterrupted use for twenty years, and your family hasn't stepped foot on this property all this time. Nor have they helped maintain the road. So if I were you, I wouldn't go around practicing law without a license. It's complicated."

"You mean too complicated for my little old feminine brain to decipher?"

"I didn't say that." Alec smothered a smile.

Amelia shot daggers at Alec. "But we paid taxes and liability insurance."

"And I made improvements on the cabin which we visibly occupied."

"Why don't you just offer to buy the land from me? You're a lawyer. I'm sure you have enough money for the transaction, and your relatives would grant you an easement." Judging from his office, she wasn't sure Billy Bob had two dimes to rub together. If he gave away his services to family members, which he probably did, there would be no real clients left to pay his fees.

"The law is the law. Why should I buy the land from you when I'm already living on it? I have no plans to move."

"I don't care what the law says. You owe me, Mr. Brady. I want you to take me on a tour of my grandmother's property. I want to walk every square inch of it, and then I want to sell it. So whatever you have to do to make that happen, work it out. Use that fancy Duke-educated legal mind of yours to come up with a solution. Do you know who the surrounding property owners are? We're going to need an easement."

"That might be difficult. I know those people. They won't grant an easement to an outsider."

"As I told you, my grandparents have owned that property for forty years. They're hardly outsiders."

"My grandfather was born in New York, but after he married my grandmother, he spent the rest of his life in Confrontation and they still considered him an outsider."

"Maybe the owners that sold this property to my grandfather in the first place would grant us an easement. He had to pay eleven heirs to get this property. Maybe the easement was part of the sale."

"I couldn't find a record of that, unless you have one."

Amelia expelled a breath and shook her head. Her grandmother's condo housed a mountain of papers, papers that would need a front-end loader to penetrate.

"My aunt might be interested in granting you an easement that would provide access to your property via a road she owns, if you would grant her one. Back in 2008, she says she wrote to your grandparents about getting a right-of-way, and it was never answered." Alec handed her a letter.

Dear Will and Katherine,

I hope this finds you both well. We are doing O.K. here. I hope you understand what I was trying to explain on the phone. There's only a short piece of your property I'd need a right away over and it's at the edge next to Jimmy Dickens. I love and appreciate you so much for helping me out. Thanks for being our friend for so many years. Take good care,

Love,

Brenna & Bill

"She left her telephone number and asked them to call, but she never heard from them."

Amelia handed the letter back to Alec.

"Isn't that the same aunt whose sister has been living in the cabin rent-free all these years? My grandfather was a very trusting person, but I think he was afraid to sign over a right-of-way. I don't think he understood the legal consequences. Land was very sacred to him. Anyway, that's only one property owner. If she turns me down, I'll need to contact the other surrounding property owners. Could you write them a letter explaining our wish to sell the property and seek an easement that would facilitate the sale?"

"My Aunt Barbara owns the adjacent lot."

"Would she be willing to entertain a reasonable offer regarding the price of such an easement that would permit access to our property through a public road via her property? Or would one of them be interesting in buying either of the tracts of land? That would allow them to add on to their property. I would be willing to consider a significantly discounted offer from the tax-appraised value."

"I spoke to the gentleman whose property is

32

adjacent to the north end of your property, and he'll offer eight thousand dollars."

"Eight thousand dollars? That property was appraised at $90,000."

"He might be willing to accept five thousand dollars. He just got married and he says he has to talk to God about it first and then his wife."

Alec held a copy of the email in his hand. Amelia grabbed it. "Let me see that. 'My neighbor informed me that land has no right of way. I growed up here and have never known of any access to that property. I am making an offer of $8,000.00.' "

Amelia rolled her eyes. "Who do you have to sleep with to get an easement around here?"

Alec's eyes widened, and he stared at her hungrily. "What are you offering?"

"That's just an expression, Mountain Man." Yikes. The sooner she got out of Dodge or Confrontation or whatever this one-horse town was called, the better off she'd be. She doubted Confrontation had even one horse.

She looked out the window. Not a cloud in the sky. So why was she shaking? She was spitting mad, that's why. Suddenly, a passing cloud obscured the sun.

"Do you see that big storm cloud out there?" Amelia's hands started to tremble.

Alec glanced up at the sky through the window.

"Seems like the only cloud around here is inside this office," Alec observed.

Amelia bristled and forgot about the weather momentarily.

"Five thousand dollars? That's ridiculous. That's not a serious offer."

"My uncle enjoys the peace and quiet of the mountains. He doesn't want a lot of noise and construction. The man above him wants to build cottages on the property, and all the construction vehicles would have to go through my uncle's property to get to their land. Uncle Bundy is as stubborn as a mule."

"Why doesn't Uncle Bundy want to sell or grant an easement? What's he hiding up here?"

"Nothing," Alec pointed out quickly. "He's just set in his ways. He's been offered a lot of money over the years, but he won't sell and he won't grant an easement. He feels that being at the end of the road gives his property significant value. He believes the real value of his property is its seclusion, which would be disturbed by the easement. He probably overvalues his property. I'm afraid the dollar signs dancing in his head are large enough that he doesn't want to risk the big payout by giving an easement.

"As far as your second piece of property, there's a widow who owns the property on the mountaintop. Her husband had always wanted to own the property you have. She's willing to offer $15,000."

"Mr. Brady, that land is worth more than a hundred thousand dollars."

"What are you going to do with it? You don't want to live here."

"Never in a million years," Amelia admitted. "My grandfather had a working spring on his property that supplied a continuous flow of water for this whole town for forty years. Don't you think it would be fair if they granted him an easement? Otherwise, I may just have to shut off the town's water supply."

34

"How are you going to do that if you can't access the property? And besides, according to the records, your grandfather granted my family water rights in perpetuity. That means their grantees, their heirs, and/or successors and assigns forever."

"I know what in perpetuity means." Amelia scowled. "What about the third landowner with property adjacent to ours?"

"His father just died, and he expects to have the property on the market by the end of April, but he would prefer that the buyer of his property make the decision about whether or not to grant the easement. And he said he'd have problems accessing the lower portion of the property due to the terrain of the land."

"I can't wait that long. But that makes no difference."

"Why not?"

"Because you are going to help me."

"I don't see that happening."

"There's something you don't know about me, Mr. Brady. I don't give up easily. You don't want to mess with me or underestimate me." Amelia bristled.

"Or what?" Alec said, smirking.

"I have a gun." Amelia patted her purse.

Alec glanced at her handbag and smiled. "And I have a rifle. What difference does that make unless you're planning to shoot me?"

Amelia crossed her arms. Jethro was growing more infuriating by the second. How could she ever have found him attractive? He might be a lawyer, but he had no idea who he was dealing with. She was not going to give up until she sold this property.

"Well, if I don't get an easement, then I might have

to sell the land to the CIA or some black ops firm so they can use it as a training ground. Maybe a shooting range. They'll have to helicopter in. That would be mighty noisy. Or maybe I'll sell it to a forest products company and let them chop down all the trees. That would certainly reduce the value of the surrounding properties. Or an oil company interested in drilling for crude. I understand that fracking is quite profitable these days."

Alec rubbed his jaw. "This is a quiet town. We'd like to keep it that way."

"More like a ghost town. Is there even a decent restaurant around here that doesn't serve hog jowls?"

"Depends on your definition of decent. The people who live here want to keep things the way they are. They don't want any Florida people or any other people trespassing on their land."

Amelia pointed to the property plat. "Trespassing? According to this deed, this is my grandmother's land. How many times do I have to tell you that?" Amelia pursed her lips. "Maybe a satanic cult would be interested in establishing a commune up here in these mountains. Or maybe…I could interest a utility company in buying the spring and start charging you all for the water you've stolen from my grandparents over the years. I can think of a lot of interesting uses for this property."

"You have quite an imagination."

"I think so. And I'm just getting started."

"Those tactics won't work with me, Miss Rushing. You can get your tight little butt out of my office and find someone else to threaten."

Amelia batted her lashes and crossed her legs. So,

he *had* noticed her. Maybe she could use his attraction to her advantage.

"Why, Mr. Brady. I do believe you're flirting with me." She pulled down her dress again to hide the spreading run in her stockings that kept appearing at the most inopportune times. A run that was quickly becoming a marathon. Now the man was openly staring at the bare spots on her legs.

"That's not flirting where I come from."

"You were born here, weren't you?"

Alec furrowed his eyebrows.

"I'll bet you were born in my grandmother's cabin."

Alec's silence spoke volumes.

"Oh, my God, you were, weren't you?"

Alec rose from his chair. "Miss Rushing, it's not a crime to be poor."

"I didn't say it was." Amelia tried to look properly shameful. "Let's settle this thing."

"I think our business is done."

Amelia walked around the desk, reached up, put a hand on Alec's shoulder, and pushed him down roughly into his chair.

"No. I think our business here has just begun. But right now I'm starving. I've been driving for hours, and I've driven around what you call a town, and I can't find a single restaurant."

"You've got to go all the way into Demming to find one."

"How far is Demming?"

"About thirty miles."

"Make us a reservation."

"Miss Rushing, I'm not a concierge. I'm a lawyer.

And a damn good one."

"If you're so good, what are you doing in this crummy office in this crummy town? And anyway, you're *my* lawyer now."

"I didn't agree to take you on as a client."

"Looks to me like you could use a client. Anyway, I'll be out of your hair soon enough. But right now my blood sugar is low and I need to eat. We need to leave before it starts to rain."

"There's no rain in the forecast. Are you always this bossy?"

"Only when I'm hungry and mad. And right now, I'm a little of both." Amelia's growling stomach betrayed her. "Okay, here's how it's going to work. I'm going to pack, check out of what you townfolk call a hotel, and I'll meet you back here."

"So you're leaving after all?"

"Who said anything about leaving? I've been thinking. Why should I waste my money on a hotel when my family owns a perfectly good cabin? I'm going to move in and stay there until you sell my property. Then tomorrow morning you can take me on a tour of my land and introduce me to the surrounding landowners."

"And if I don't?"

"I'm going to cause you a world of trouble."

"You wouldn't do that."

"Watch me, Jethro."

$$****$$

The problem was Alec couldn't *stop* watching her. From the moment he'd entered his office and taken one look at Amelia Rushing, he was "gobsmacked," as his mama used to say. She'd always told him that's how true love happens. And this woman wasn't even his type. She was a little spitfire. Probably super-high maintenance, like the women he'd dated in New York. If he wasn't careful, he could fall hard for her. Even that giant run in her stocking was turning him on.

It had been a while since he'd been attracted to a woman. The truth was there weren't really any eligible women in Confrontation except Brady cousins, and they were strictly off limits. There had been women in New York, but he didn't live in New York now, and he didn't envision himself going back to that rat race. Anyway, he didn't know any women who would give up the big city to live in his small hometown. He was satisfied with his lifestyle, but he did miss the companionship of a woman. There was no sense thinking about this particular woman since, when her business was concluded here, she'd be gone. It was obvious she was itching to get out of town. Probably back to her boyfriend. A woman who looked like Amelia Rushing would definitely have a boyfriend, maybe even a husband, although she wasn't wearing a wedding ring.

He couldn't imagine a beautiful, vibrant woman like Amelia Rushing—with her fall of luxurious, sable hair that he couldn't wait to get his hands into, silky white skin, kissable lips, and bedroom eyes—being content living in Confrontation. Unless he could convince her to stay. Or hogtie her. That might be interesting. That would be the typical behavior of a male in Confrontation, although it wasn't his style. More like Uncle Bunnell's, if you could believe the stories. And he was nothing like Uncle Bunnell. It was easier to hate her, since he knew he could never have her. His feelings for her were complex and confusing. She accused him of flirting. Well, he wanted to do a lot more than that with the beautiful realtor.

She had a lot of nerve showing up and announcing she was moving into his cabin. Well, technically it *was* her cabin, or at least her grandmother's cabin. But still, where was she supposed to sleep? In his mother's old room?

Somehow, he'd been hoodwinked into taking her out to dinner. How had that happened? During dinner, he would calmly explain the situation and talk her out of her plan. He was a champion debater. He couldn't afford to have her stay on the property. Who knew what she'd discover? He'd heard stories about the Rushing property his whole life. Stories about his Uncle Bunnell, nicknamed "Uncle Bundy" after the notorious serial killer Ted Bundy. All he knew was that, over the years, people in his life kept disappearing. The stories were probably exaggerated, but he couldn't afford to take that chance. He was going to have to figure out how to get rid of her before she learned the ugly truth about Confrontation.

Chapter Four

Amelia was out of breath after the strenuous walk from the car. She looked back down the road.

"That's a pretty steep driveway," she observed, mustering all her strength to fight her way through the underbrush. "I think we need a machete." Her legs were practically stripped bare by the briars, leaving multiple jagged holes in her stockings. There were too many runs to cover up. She couldn't help but notice Alec Brady staring at them. He'd probably been imagining her naked all through dinner. Well, hell, she had been mentally undressing him, too. Apparently, she had lost all sense of modesty. She couldn't wait to sink her teeth into him, after a proper bath. If this cabin even had indoor plumbing.

"You wanted to walk the property. You know you could have looked at aerial photos of the property without leaving your living room. Despite the low opinion you seem to have of our town, the county is pretty tech-savvy. Everything's online. You could have called the county property mapping office and got what you needed."

With only a small incline to go, Amelia put on the brakes like a petulant child and refused to move.

Alec relented, taking Amelia's hand. "Here, let me help you."

When he touched her hand, her skin sizzled. She

almost drew it back, but she didn't. It felt good in hers. They walked hand in hand uphill for a few more minutes—actually Alec pulled her up—until a modest wooden cabin appeared in the clearing. When he dropped her hand, all the warmth left her body. Night was about to fall, and she was feeling the cold, feeling out of breath and way out of shape. The tips of her nipples were protruding through her short-sleeved T-shirt. And Alec was politely trying NOT to stare at them.

"Maybe I'd better carry you over the threshold since you don't have legal access to the place." Left unsaid was the fact that she wasn't sure she could make it across the threshold on her own steam.

Amelia frowned. "That won't be necessary." Irritated, she met his challenge and managed to summon a burst of energy and follow Alec in when he opened the door with his key.

Amelia's eyes widened and her mouth opened as she stood at the door in amazement.

"For some reason I thought this was going to be a two-room shack with a potbellied stove, covered with layers of dust and a million creepy crawly things." She looked around. "Doesn't look like much from the outside. But inside it looks more like something out of *Better Homes & Gardens®*.

Alec smiled proudly. "How long has it been since you've been up here?"

"This is my first time. But I've seen pictures, lots of pictures, and this doesn't look anything like the snapshots my grandmother showed me. Their cabin was made of wood, with a screened-in porch. And it was small. The kitchen floors were linoleum, not pine. The appliances were old-fashioned and white."

Amelia walked the length of the cabin. "Wow, you actually have good taste."

"For a hillbilly?"

Amelia shrugged.

"I've made some improvements. I'm pretty good with my hands."

Amelia looked at Alec's strong hands and slapped herself silently for her traitorous thoughts about what else he might be good at. She was definitely horny, and she hoped he wasn't too observant.

"Let me show you around the rest of the place."

Alec led her on a tour of the house, from the modern, fully-equipped and stocked kitchen to two cozy bedrooms, modern bathrooms, and back to the living room with a million-dollar view of the mountains. The sun was beginning to set, surrounding the mountains in a riot of color.

"And there wasn't a picture window in the snapshots."

"I had it installed," Alec observed. "Being a realtor, you'd know all about upgrades."

Amelia stopped in front of a painting of a woman. It was arresting, and she couldn't look away. The colors were wonderful. The style of this painting reminded her of the one in her grandmother's condo, but her grandmother's was a landscape.

"Who is this woman?"

"That was my mama when she was younger."

"She was a beautiful woman. No, she was more than beautiful. She was absolutely stunning."

Amelia moved closer to the painting and studied the signature. "That's a Moss Hathaway."

"It's just a painting."

"A Moss Hathaway is not *just* a painting. If you knew anything about art, you'd know that. Didn't they teach you anything at Duke? Do you know how much this painting is worth? Since Moss Hathaway disappeared without a trace, his paintings, if you could find them, are priceless. My grandmother has one."

Alec led her away from the living room. "It's probably just a copy. If this painting had been worth anything, my mother would have sold it to pay for my education. As it was, she sent me what she could, but I had to work my way through college and law school. I'm still paying back the loans."

That disclosure only made Amelia more attracted to Alec. She liked a self-reliant man.

Amelia inspected the painting. "I majored in art history in college. I've seen Moss Hathaways in museums here and abroad. I know the real thing when I see it. How did you come to own a Moss Hathaway? Dealers all over the world would kill to snag one of these. There must be a story there."

"It's nobody's business." It was obvious he didn't want to talk about the authenticity of the painting or his recently departed mother.

She tried a gentler tack. "Thanks for fixing up my house."

"It's my house," Alec objected. "Possession is nine-tenths of the law."

"You don't really believe that, do you?"

"Your grandmother hasn't been back here in decades."

"She couldn't get back. Arguing with me is pointless. Where do you want me to sleep?"

"Are you seriously going to move in here?"

"Right after you get my suitcase out of the car."

Alec shook his head. "Do I look like a butler?"

Amelia relented and assumed a less demanding tone. "I'd appreciate it if you would please get my suitcase from the car. It's dark out there."

"If you're afraid of the dark, then you sure don't want to live in a cabin in the woods."

"If you help me sell the place, then I won't have to, will I?"

Raising his hands in frustration, Alec turned and started to the car. "I'll be right back. Watch out for the creepy crawly things and bears. And you can sleep in Ma's old room, first door on the left."

Bears? This had been a bad idea from the start. The prospect of sleeping in the room of a recently deceased woman was less than thrilling. But she wasn't afraid of ghosts—just bad weather. Hopefully, the weather would hold. The thought of surviving a storm in the mountains was chilling. With all these tall trees—lightning rods—surrounding the house. And the idea of thunder crashing about against the mountains was frightening. At least she wouldn't be alone. She'd have Alec. He doubted her resolve, but she would show him what she was made of. She was going to put down roots until the sale went through. No matter how long it took. Even if she had to become a temporary resident of Confrontation. And she was beginning to come to terms with the town. It was small and insular but at the same time beautiful and mysterious. And it was surprisingly appealing, like her new roommate.

While Alec ambled to the car to get her suitcase, she looked around her new bedroom. There were twelve—she counted them—afghans folded neatly on a queen-sized bed. It must get cold up in the mountains, or else Alec's mother was a hoarder. What had she died of? Amelia opened a drawer and found more than twenty hair combs.

A few minutes later, Alec wandered in and placed her suitcase on a French provincial makeup table. Caught in the act of snooping, Amelia slammed the dresser drawer shut.

"Sorry," she managed.

"I'm sure you have questions," Alec said.

"None of my business."

"I haven't changed anything about the room since she passed."

"That's understandable."

"You must be wondering…"

Amelia shrugged.

"Alzheimer's. Early onset. Well, in the end, pneumonia is what she died of."

That explained the abundance of afghans and combs.

"You took care of her yourself?"

"Her sisters and my cousins came by during the day. I had her at night. We don't put our elderly in homes like you Florida people do."

Amelia bristled. "How do you know what we do?"

"It's what I've heard."

"My grandmother took care of my grandfather without help until the end. It was hard on her, but we take care of our own, too." Amelia hoped he'd never find out about her father's intention to put his mother into an independent living facility.

"I didn't mean anything by it."

Alec handed her a folded set of freshly laundered, sweet-smelling flowered sheets. "I'd have made the bed, but we weren't expecting company."

Amelia took the sheets out of Alec's hands, brushing against his fingers, and received another electric shock—a lightning-like sensation. Alec's use of the word "we," probably out of habit, indicated he still hadn't accepted that his mother was gone.

"When you're ready for bed, come on out to the living room. I'll make you a cup of hot cocoa."

"You don't need to wait on me."

"Ma couldn't sleep before she had her cup of hot cocoa. Otherwise, she'd wander around the house all night."

Amelia looked at Alec. The man was full of surprises. He was sweet, a nurturer. Nothing like she'd originally thought him. She accepted his generous gesture.

"That would be nice."

Amelia slipped into a cornflower-blue silk nightgown, a silk robe, and her favorite pair of snuggly grey UGG slippers and walked into the cozy living room. A fire was burning. She noticed some bestsellers on the shelves on either side of the fireplace—even some romances. Either Alec was a voracious reader or his mother had been. Amelia read two or three books a week, and she recognized some of her favorite titles.

Alec came up behind her. "Did you think I was illiterate?"

"The thought never crossed my mind." The man was wickedly perceptive.

Alec had set out a tray of hot chocolate and home-baked cookies.

"Go ahead, have some," he offered. "I baked them myself. Ma had a sweet tooth. It's been kind of lonely since she's been gone."

"I thought you had a big family."

"I do. And they're always stopping by unexpectedly. But there's lonely and there's lonely. It's like I don't know what to do with myself anymore. My mother was such a big part of my life, and suddenly it's just me. I had so much responsibility and now nothing. It's an empty feeling, like part of me is missing."

Amelia sat down on the couch and took a sip of the hot liquid. Alec had put marshmallows in the chocolate, and they tasted gooey and delicious, warming her insides.

"Mmm."

Alec reached over and gently brushed her top lip. Her entire body tingled, and she pulled back.

"Sorry," he apologized. "I saw you had a milk moustache. Hazards of being a caregiver."

There were worse things he could be, Amelia thought, settling down. She couldn't stop thinking about his fingers on her lips and wondered how they'd feel on other parts of her body. It was crazy. She'd only known Alec for a few short hours, and yet she couldn't stop thinking about him. His presence had some kind of magnetic effect on her. Just looking at him generated a positive electric charge, like their ions were colliding.

"It's all right. It's nice. Thank you." What other things would she learn about this man? And what difference did it make, since Confrontation would soon be in her rearview mirror?

"Thanks for dinner tonight," Amelia said gratefully.

"It wasn't so bad, was it?"

Amelia smiled. "Honestly, it was much better than I expected."

"What were you expecting? Hog jowls and squirrel?"

Amelia laughed. Actually, that was exactly what she had expected. What she got was one of the best gourmet dinners she'd ever tasted. The menu was varied, some game items, fresh mountain trout, pastas, delicious vegetables. And some rather pleasant company. They'd talked about their college experiences, growing up in a small town versus a large city, travel, everything and nothing. She liked listening to his voice. She felt comfortable in his presence. He had impeccable manners. He was polite to the wait staff. Unlike What's-His-Name, who refused to thank a server who refilled their water glasses because it was "his job." What's-His-Name looked at life as a hierarchy, with him on the top rung. The truth was he was just plain rude and obnoxious.

When the check came, Alec had paid it, graciously and with a generous tip. But not because the server was beautiful and big-busted (which she was). What was it about servers? Alec didn't seem to notice the way the server looked or the way she was built. He was focused like a laser on his dinner date the entire time. Unlike What's-His-Name. She imagined Alec didn't have a cheating bone in his entire body. And he seemed more sensitive, more in touch with his feelings than What's-His-Name had ever been. That was a good thing, in her opinion.

"One of the losing contestants on *Top Chef* opened the restaurant. I'd stack it up against any I've tried in

New York."

"I've never actually been to New York," Amelia admitted.

"Who's the hick now?" Alec challenged.

Okay, she deserved that. "How long did you live in New York?"

"For about three years after law school, when I was working for that big firm I told you about. I was on partner track. That city has a lot to offer, but honestly I was never so glad to get back home. The pace is too hectic up there. I had forgotten how comforting quiet can be. Confrontation is more my speed."

Amelia bit back a comment. Alec was obviously prejudiced against so-called "Florida people." He considered them snobs. Maybe he was right. She had been just as narrow-minded about what she considered "hicks" from North Carolina. The conversation at dinner had been stimulating. He had been a pleasant dinner companion. Her initial impression of Alec Brady was inaccurate. He was anything but a hick. Her attraction to him had grown exponentially over the course of the evening.

"So, what's on tap for tomorrow?" she asked expectantly, realizing that she was looking forward to spending more time with the country lawyer.

"Well, I thought we could drive around your two tracts of land. I could introduce you to some of your neighbors. Maybe if they meet you in person they'll change their mind about granting you an easement or buying your property."

"What are the chances of that happening?"

"Doubtful."

"Maybe you could talk to some of them. Since

you're all related."

"That's not likely. There's a lot of bad blood in Confrontation, even among family."

"Like the Hatfields and the McCoys?"

"Worse. The Bradys hold serious grudges."

"About what?"

"Well, my Uncle Bundy Brady is wanted in three states for murder. He's a serial killer, he's on the loose, and I don't think it's safe for strangers to be anywhere around here. I think you'd better leave as soon as possible."

"You're not going to scare me away with your tall tales, Mr. Brady."

"Take your chances, then. Don't say I didn't warn you. Just keep your bedroom door locked."

"Why? Do you wander around at night?"

Alec took a good long look at her.

"I just might be tempted, if I see something I like." He licked some hot chocolate from his lips, and she shuddered in response like a Pavlovian dog. Game on, Billy Bob.

Suddenly, her fancy negligee seemed flimsy and she pulled her robe tighter around her practically naked body and her visibly hardening nipples. She felt exposed. Jethro was getting too close for comfort. And talk about tempting. All thoughts of proper behavior went up in smoke through the fireplace whenever she looked into his dreamy blue eyes. She finished her hot chocolate, trying not to think about Alec's tongue tangling with hers, and placed the cup gingerly on the tray.

"Thank you. I'm going to go to bed now. See you in the morning." She half hoped he'd stop her, but he didn't.

"Sleep tight. Don't let the bedbugs bite."

Amelia's eyes widened. "You have bedbugs?"

"Just something Ma used to say before she put me to sleep."

A flash of lightning crackled electrifyingly outside the picture window. Instinctively she jumped up into Alec's arms.

He caught her and held her as if she were weightless. "Hey, it's only heat lightning. That just means it's lightning that's too far away to be heard."

"But the storm may be moving in our direction." She tightened her arms around Alec's neck. "I'd better check my weather radar app."

"You don't need a weather app to tell a storm's coming. Just look up at the sky, see the way the wind is blowing through the trees. You can smell a storm coming. You're not scared of a little lightning, are you?"

He had no idea. The last thing she wanted was for him to find out about all her phobias. "Do you know how many people get struck by lightning every year?"

"I have a feeling you're going to tell me."

"You have approximately a one in 1,749,851 chance of getting killed by lightning in North Carolina every year," Amelia stated. "And Americans are twice as likely to die a lightning-related death as from a tornado, hurricane, or flood."

"That's obscure."

"I looked it up before I came here. You'd be surprised. At least it's nighttime. Seventy percent of all lightning injuries and fatalities occur in the afternoon. You've got a lot of tall trees around here. The average lightning strike is six miles long."

Amelia ventured a nervous look out the window just after a particularly loud crack of thunder. Lightning illuminated the sky, and she stared into the face of a crusty-looking, bearded mountain man. She screamed and pointed at the picture window, nearly causing Alec to drop her.

"There's a scary-looking man in the window."

"Did he have a beard? And red hair?"

Amelia nodded her head frantically.

"Uncle Bundy. He's always popping up. He knows he's safe around here."

"You're harboring a serial killer?"

"He's my uncle. He claims he's innocent. And they haven't found any bodies yet."

"Well, now, that makes me feel a whole lot better. I *will* be locking my bedroom door tonight. You act like seeing a serial killer is just your everyday occurrence, and that being a serial killer is a run-of-the-mill occupation."

Alec shrugged as he carried Amelia into her bedroom and deposited her on the bed.

Thunder reverberated around the room. It was getting louder. The storm was growing in intensity.

Amelia jumped up again and landed back in Alec's arms.

"Okay, that was not heat lightning."

Alec smiled and snuggled her closer. "I know I'm irresistible, sugar, but it's just a little storm. Nothing to worry about."

"Nothing to worry about?" Amelia said. "We're out here in the middle of nowhere."

"Our summer storms are spectacular. I like a good

storm. It's comforting. Helps me sleep." He looked at her with hooded eyes. Crinkling his nose, he rubbed it against hers, bringing his lips dangerously close to hers. Her body responded.

What was he, an Eskimo? What was this "sugar" talk? Was it just a mountain term of endearment? Did he refer to every girl he met as "sugar"? And how many girls had there been? Was it a long line? And why didn't he just kiss her already? Before she exploded or dispensed with ceremony and attacked him.

"Storms are anything but comforting," Amelia said. "What if one of those giant trees crashes through the picture window?"

"What if a meteor lands outside the front door?"

"It could happen."

"You ever see anybody about your problem?"

"What problem?"

"Your fear of storms."

Amelia's cheeks reddened. "It's just a healthy respect for Mother Nature. Completely normal."

"No, I think it goes way beyond that. You're afraid of rain, storms, and lightning. Unnaturally afraid, to the point of obsession."

"I'm not obsessed," Amelia objected. Was she that obvious?

"You haven't taken your nose out of that weather radar app since you got here."

Alec sat down on the bed, cradling her in his arms, steadying her hands. "Miss Rushing, calm down, please, and look at me. It's going to be okay. I promise. And if you get scared in the middle of the night, you can always crawl into bed with me. My door's always open."

Amelia's jaw dropped. "Is that an invitation?"

"Do you want it to be?"

"Don't say anything you don't mean," she said, raising her chin, wishing with all her might that he'd kiss her and get it over with. The tension was killing her.

"I never do. I just want you to know that I'll keep you safe."

Amelia blew out a breath. She almost believed him. He certainly was strong. Strong enough to protect her. But who would protect her from him? Sitting this close on his lap, she could feel his erection. She was certain about one thing. Nothing about this house or this town or this night or this man was okay.

****

Alec paced the living room. He was never going to be able to get any sleep now. What he needed was a cold shower. Amelia had felt so vulnerable in his arms. She was a stubborn woman, but underneath that crocodile demeanor was a warm and passionate woman. He'd stake his career on it—such as it was. Holding her close on his lap, he'd ached for her, and he thought he'd detected the same raw need in her eyes. He'd wanted to kiss her, more than anything, to taste those luscious lips of hers.

But he didn't want to scare her off by moving too quickly. She had awakened something in him that had lain dormant since he'd come back to Confrontation. It had been a long time since he'd held a woman. And it felt good. She felt good. Her nightgown didn't leave much to the imagination. She was feisty but at the same time fragile. He hadn't wanted to let her go. He wanted to get to know her better. But she couldn't have made it plainer that she was in a hurry to leave. And that she thought he was a hick, or worse. She hadn't given Confrontation a chance. If she had, she might find a reason to stay. Maybe he'd give her a reason to stay. With all the thoughts swirling around in his head, it was going to be a long night.

Chapter Five

Amelia had the best sleep she'd had in years. Must be the sweet mountain air. And the sweet dreams she was having about Alec Brady. She was more of an ocean girl, but the sounds and the scents in the mountains were intoxicating. The storm had moved out, replaced by the friendly sounds of crickets, hoot owls, and tree frogs. She thought she'd locked her bedroom door, but while she was asleep Alec must have come in and opened the windows. Cool air that smelled like pine-scented bath crystals filled the room, swamping her senses. She snuggled under one of the comforters. She was beginning to understand why her grandparents had bought the place and why they used to love visiting. But then why had they stopped coming here so abruptly thirty years ago? It didn't make any sense.

Stretching lazily, she swung her legs over the edge of the bed and pushed her feet into a pair of fuzzy slippers, padded toward the bathroom, and screamed.

A girl with frizzy red hair and wearing a skimpy bikini walked out of the bedroom next door, followed by a giant wolf.

"We ain't interested in giving you a right away." The girl fixed her with a frigid stare.

"Who are you?"

"Marie Antoinette Brady. Alec's cousin. Heard there was a Florida person snooping around our property."

"Actually, it's my property, but it's for sale."

"You can't sell this property. This is my home."

Amelia blew out a breath.

"You live here too?"

"Sometimes."

"Who else lives here?"

"Cousin Alec is a soft touch. He takes in strays."

Amelia stared at the wolf. "Does he bite?"

"Only if he's hungry." Marie Antoinette blew her straight face and started laughing.

"I'm beginning to get the picture. Any girls ever stay over?"

Marie Antoinette laughed. "Why. You jealous?"

"No, of course not. I hardly know the man."

"Are you Alec's new girlfriend?"

"No, I'm his client, and this is actually my house, or rather, my grandmother's house."

"You're one of them Florida people. I knew it. I knew it the moment I seen you."

"I live in Florida, but I don't know why you would call me that."

"We don't like them Florida people. They's uppity."

Alec strolled into the bathroom, and Marie Antoinette spun around.

"Jesus, Lord have mercy, you scared me to death."

"Why don't you call on someone you know," Alec teased.

"The plumbing's broke at my house. I'm going to take a shower."

"In your bathing suit? How did you get in?"

"I came in through Aunt Necey's window."

"You could have used the front door. You should have called first. I have company."

"I ken see that. Phone's busted because of the storm."

Alec scratched his head. "And you shouldn't be walking around in a storm anyway."

"I was scared."

Amelia stepped back and mutely pointed to the animal before she could speak.

"S-she has a wolf."

Alec didn't seemed bothered by the furry intruder.

"You know how that dog sheds. Now I'm going to have dog hairs all over the place."

"Sorry. Dr. Landrew and I will be out of your way in about an hour. Then you and your *girlfriend* can have the house all to yourself to do the nasty."

"Marie Antoinette Brady, watch your mouth, or I'll wash it out with soap. Miss Rushing is a lady, and she's not used to talk like that. Remember what I told you about acting civilized around guests."

Marie Antoinette hung her head.

"Remember, you were named after a beautiful French empress," Alec said.

"Who got her head chopped off for eating cake," remarked Marie Antoinette.

Alec sighed. "That's not exactly how it happened. Just mind your manners."

"I'll try, Cousin Alec."

Amelia stared at the wolf. "Who's Dr. Landrew?"

"She's my dog. I named her after my gynecologist."

Amelia blinked. Although Marie Antoinette was well developed and almost every one of her ample

59

assets was on display for Alec and all the world to see, the girl didn't look old enough to have a gynecologist. But, in these parts, who knew? Amelia mentally kicked herself for stooping to stereotypes again. But she couldn't help it if her mind ran wild with thoughts of improper behavior. For all she knew, Alec was sleeping with his cousin. She certainly seemed comfortable enough around him, and she was available. In fact, an obvious hero-worship vibe emanated from the little diva.

"Are you sure Dr. Landrew is not a wolf?"

"He may be," answered Marie Antoinette, her eyes sparkling.

"And she's not my girlfriend," Alec insisted.

"That ain't what Daddy said."

"You talked to Uncle Bundy?"

"He's jes passin' through. Don't tell no one. You promise?"

Alec sighed. "Don't worry. What did he have to say for himself? "

"Daddy said he seen you with a girl last night."

"Amelia is just staying here for a few days until we get her land situation straightened out."

"I saw him digging around the graveyard. He says when it rains the ground is nice and soft. Perfect weather for burying bodies."

"You didn't see him actually bury a body, did you?"

"I seen the shovel, and he smelt awful, like rot. I asked him to stay and he said he couldn't. He's on the run again. He said he was going to stay at your house, so I followed him over here, but he must have gotten spooked when he seen that girl on your lap through the picture window. Since she was in Aunt Necey's bed, I just slept on the couch."

Amelia shuddered and imagined how she would have felt waking up next to a half-dressed mountain girl and her wolf.

"Okay, go on and get yourself something to eat and put on some clothes. I've got some bacon and eggs frying on the stove."

Amelia turned to face Alec. "Are you running a bed and breakfast here?"

"Marie Antoinette's family. She's like my sister. Her daddy's gone all the time, so she doesn't have anyone to watch out for her. Mama used to care for her, but since she's been sick, I'm all Marie Antoinette's got."

"Marie is Bundy's daughter?" Amelia asked. "But she's so young, and he's, well, a lot older. How did that happen?"

Alec laughed. "I'm guessing the usual way."

"That's not what I mean."

"Uncle Bundy's wife was not much older than Marie Antoinette is now when she married him. She was a real beauty. He went off on a drinking binge one weekend, and when he came home he had Aunt Shelley with him. He moved her into his cabin. Said they were married. Not long after that she became pregnant, and Marie Antoinette was born. Aunt Shelley had a passion for all things French."

"Where's Aunt Shelley now?" I asked, following Alec and Marie Antoinette into the kitchen and sitting at the table.

"We don't know. Marie said she heard them fighting one night, and then Aunt Shelley just disappeared. No one ever saw her again. My mom took Marie in, tried to look after the girl, but then when she got sick Marie just started running wild. I'm trying to rein her in, teach her some things, help her make the right decisions about life."

"You said you felt responsible for Marie. You mean like a sister?"

"She's my cousin, but yes."

"Alec, what do you think happened to your Aunt Shelley?"

Alec looked away. "I don't know. She just disappeared."

"Do you think your Uncle Bundy could have had something to do with his wife's disappearance?"

Alec shrugged. "I'm not for certain. I need to run to the office to take care of some things. Eat your breakfast. I'll be back, and then I'll show you the rest of the property, and we'll meet some of the landowners."

Amelia narrowed her eyes. "Don't think I'm falling for your Mr. Nice Guy routine just because you made me breakfast. And don't keep me waiting too long."

"You came here loaded for bear. I think you need an attitude adjustment."

"Is that a threat?" Amelia shifted in her seat, heat permeating her body. Somehow, Alec managed to make that pronouncement sound vaguely sexual. The country lawyer was beginning to make her uncomfortable in more ways than one.

Chapter Six

Relaxing on the hammock, suspended in utter silence and pleasure, Amelia finally understood her grandfather's desire to build his home in the mountains among trees as far as the eye could see, with restful scenic views of the valley, clear cool mountain streams, and towering mountain ranges. Away from the humidity, grit, and grating traffic noise of Miami and Fort Lauderdale. Away from the stress. With year-round delightful climate. Cool summer nights, mountain wildflowers, twittering birds. It was an idyllic spot. If she wasn't careful, she'd fall under what her grandmother called the spell of the mountains.

Amelia pulled out her iPhone to check her e-mails. There was no Internet connection. Of course. They were in Bradyville. Her thoughts moved on. There was something about that painting. She'd studied Moss Hathaway in art class. He'd disappeared some thirty years ago. The details were a little murky. She couldn't wait to Google him.

She walked into the house and tried to access the Internet again. This time she got a connection. There were a number of entries. She selected the top one and began reading:

Landscape Painter Moss Hathaway
Disappears Without a Trace
The art world is stunned by the disappearance of

well-known painter Moss Hathaway, 40, who vanished without a trace on a painting excursion in the rural North Carolina mountains. He is presumed dead, but his body has never been found. His car was abandoned in the small town of Confrontation. Local authorities suspect foul play in this unsolved mystery of his disappearance. He is survived by his wife, Eleanore Mays Hathaway.

"Moss Hathaway was one of the greatest painters of this century," noted longtime friend and Swan House Gallery owner Reid Pickett, who represented Moss Hathaway's work in the United States. "It was not uncommon for Moss to go on unscheduled sketching trips, but he always kept in contact with Eleanore or his friends. He traveled extensively throughout the United States and Europe in search of subjects and inspiration. The art world will mourn his loss. It is a tragedy to lose someone at such an early age, especially someone of the stature of Moss Hathaway. We will all feel his loss."

The watercolorist and oil painter was at the peak of his career when he disappeared. Moss Hathaway has often been compared to the British romantic landscape painter J.M.W. Turner in his use of color and light.

Amelia stopped reading when her eye fell on the picture of the painter in the article. The man staring back was handsome as any movie star, with the most beautiful blue eyes. He looked vaguely familiar, but then of course he would. She had studied his work in college.

She looked up Eleanore Mays Hathaway. The young widow had remarried soon after her husband was declared legally dead but never had any children. How sad that she'd died never knowing what had happened to her first husband.

Amelia looked at the date on the article and frowned. That was thirty years ago. Her grandparents had been at the cabin around that time. She dialed her grandmother. Maybe she remembered something. Her grandmother had good days and bad days. Hopefully, this would be a good day.

"Hello."

"Grandma, it's Amelia."

"Hello, dear. How are things going up there? Have you made any progress?"

"Not really. Things are moving slowly. But I'm determined to stay here until everything is resolved. Don't worry."

"I'm not worried at all. I know my land is in good hands."

"Grandma, you wouldn't recognize the place if you saw it again. Alec has made so many improvements. It looks nothing like the pictures. But speaking of pictures, there is a breathtaking portrait of a woman hanging on the wall of the, well, I can hardly call it a cabin now, it's changed so much. But the portrait—it's of a beautiful woman, Necey Brady, Alec Brady's mother. It's by Moss Hathaway. The same man who painted the cabin picture hanging in your condo. Do you know anything about that? Do you remember seeing it when you were here last?"

Amelia was met with stony silence.

"Grandma? Are you still there? Is something wrong? Were you up here around the time that Moss Hathaway disappeared? Moss Hathaway was a landscape artist. He wasn't known for his portraits. But the color, the style, and the energy of your painting remind me of this picture in the cabin."

"Yes," the voice on the other end of the line whispered. "He stayed at our cabin."

"What?" Amelia shouted. "Speak louder. I can hardly hear you."

"He used our cabin to paint and to—"

"He stayed in your cabin? Are you serious? That's amazing. You know, he just disappeared one day. The police never found out what happened to him. Grandma, do you know anything about that?"

"Well, I—"

"Grandma, what aren't you telling me?"

"You have to promise not to tell a living soul."

"Grandma, how can I promise not to tell something if I don't know what it is I'm promising?"

"You'll just have to trust me."

"Please, just tell me."

"Moss Hathaway was the most handsome man I'd ever seen. Movie-star handsome. And the most kind and gentle person. His eyes were the most beautiful shade of blue. And he—"

"He what, Grandma?" Amelia coaxed. Something was bothering her grandmother, and she was determined to find out what it was.

"When he came to us all those years ago, he was exhausted. He said he needed to rest. He hadn't painted in months, and he came to the mountains to get away from it all—his fame, the publicity, the failure of his marriage. He just wanted to paint again. It was more of a need than a want."

"Go on."

"Well, his car had broken down at the foot of the

mountain, and he walked the path to our cabin. The poor man was so worn out, we said he could spend the night. Of course, I had no idea who he was at the time. The very next morning, Necey Brady came over and brought us some fresh eggs from their chickens, and that was it. Moss Hathaway was a married man, and of course Necey was so young, barely seventeen, just a child herself, but when he saw her, it was like a lightning strike. They couldn't help themselves.

"Your grandfather and I let them use our cabin to paint and to be together, away from her father and her brother. Ben Brady, Necey's father, was very strict. He didn't let his girls out much. He was very protective, to the point of obsession. Her older brother, Bunnell, was the same way. And they kept the triplets pretty much under lock and key. The girls were home schooled, and no one thought of sending them off to college. Bunnell was insane. He was so jealous of Necey and wouldn't let any man near her. Of course, she was a beautiful woman, a treasure, and any man would have been interested.

"We let her, let them, sleep there, and he painted the most wonderful portraits of her, of the mountains. He said it was some of the best work he'd ever done. Necey was his inspiration. He called her his muse. They were so happy and so in love."

"How long did this relationship go on?"

"For months. She was going to run away with him. She'd packed two suitcases, and when Bunnell was drunk, she slipped away to be with Moss."

"Eventually, Bunnell woke up, and when he found his sister gone, he was furious. He must have found out where she was from one of Necey's sisters. He probably beat the poor girl within an inch of her life before she would betray Necey's trust.

"He pounded on the door of our cabin like a madman. I think he was half mad. He broke down the door and caught them together. He pulled Necey out of bed in her negligee, slapped her around, and dragged Moss out of the bedroom and into the living room and—"

"And what, Grandma."

Amelia could hear heavy breathing over the phone.

"Grandma, are you crying?"

"It's nothing. I've got to go, honey."

"But you didn't finish the story. I need to know what happened."

"It's best to keep the past in the past." Her grandmother hung up the phone abruptly. Amelia redialed her number, but there was no answer.

Amelia went back into Necey's room and looked through her bureau drawers. She didn't know what she was looking for. Proof, but what kind of proof? And proof of what? Nothing in the dresser drawers and closets but clothes. Clothes Alec hadn't been able to give away. She looked on shelves, through books, even under the rug. Then she saw a hatbox on the top shelf of the closet, pushed all the way to the back. Inside, tied with a blue ribbon, were letters. She pulled out the packet of letters, closed the bedroom door, and began reading the private correspondence from a ghost to a ghost, love letters that hadn't seen the light of day for more than three decades.

Part II

Necey and Moss: Love Letters

Chapter Seven

Summer 1985

Miss Necey,

The first time I caught a glimpse of you standing there in the summer light, in your pearly white shift, your beautiful blonde hair flowing down to your waist, your dancing blue eyes as deep as the ocean, I swore I was looking at an angel. I thought I had gone to heaven. But my two feet were planted solidly on the ground.

Right then and there, I knew I had to paint you. Had to have you.

And I knew God landed me in this perfect place to find you.

To love you.

My angel.

I was lost when I came here, truly lost, but now I know I've been waiting my whole life for you. I am not free to love you yet, but I could no sooner stop my heart from reaching out to yours than I could stop a comet from streaking across the heavens. Now that I've found you, I am finally home.

I wish I could fathom what is going on in that marvelous mind of yours. Your shy smile puts Mona Lisa to shame and seems to tell me all I need to know.

I can only hope that you return my feelings.

I think true love comes around only once in life,

my dearest Necey. You are my chance, and I will take it.

You are an artist's dream. May I paint you? Will you sit for me? I would immortalize you.

Truly Yours, Moss Hathaway

~*~

Mr. Hathaway,

You paint a pretty picture with your words of love. I came to deliver a basketful of eggs and happened on a Romeo who would court his Juliette. I'll let you in on a little secret. My heart soars when I look at you. I can hardly catch my breath, and I've only just walked across the way. I truly don't know what's come over me. When I look at you I feel like I'm floating. My stomach does flip-flops. You stir up feelings I can't explain and don't know what to do with. My pulse races, and I can't wait to see you again.

Yes, I will sit for you. I will come to you tonight when the moon is full, if I can get away. When I come again I will see whether my mind is playing tricks, whether you still have that effect on my heart that you had on our first meet, or whether I just imagined you.

Necey

~*~

My darling Necey,

One sitting couldn't possibly satisfy me now that I've gotten a taste of you. One lifetime couldn't be enough to look into your glorious face, to gaze into your bottomless blue eyes, to capture your ethereal spirit on my canvas. Come again, my angel, and again until I have looked my fill of you. But I fear that will never happen.

Yours forever, Moss Hathaway

~*~

Mr. Hathaway…Moss,

When I stood before you and you touched me, slowly lowering the robe from my body, to position me just so for my portrait, I ached for your fingertips to touch me where I've never been touched. To follow the path of your greedy eyes. I hardly know you, but somehow I know your touch would not be rough and controlling but gentle and easy. And that you would never hurt me.

I know I have finally found peace. I have finally come alive. You were close, but I wanted you to come closer. Is that love or lust?

Whatever it is I'm feeling, I trust you. I cannot turn away, and I cannot go back.

I will see you tomorrow when the light breaks at dawn.

Yours, Necey

~*~

My dearest Necey,

Could it be that you feel about me the way I feel about you? Can you feel my heart beating with every stroke of my brush? It's pounding like a drum.

You are my muse. With you by my side, I can paint again, I can create. I am whole.

When I was arranging your robe, my fingers wandered and, in my mind, I touched your breasts and you sighed and melted into my arms. I think that was a dream. I want to make it a reality. When can you come again to the cabin? When can you come to me, my sweetest love?

Moss

~*~

Dear Moss,

My father and brother will be away for the day tomorrow morning. That would be a good time to come. I will be there at the light of day.

Your willing subject, Necey

Necey

I came across the dirt road to the Rushing place on my daily egg delivery. It was my favorite time of the morning. Mrs. Rushing loves our fresh eggs, and I love making her happy. She's such a wonderful woman. I can tell her anything. She reminds me of how my mama might have been before she got so worn out raising babies and had no time for private talks.

It was an ordinary day. The sun was shining, spreading light over the mountainside. When I approached the house, a strange man was outside working at an easel. His back was turned to me. He was concentrating on the cabin and the mountain in the distance and the way the light danced against the foliage. I took the opportunity to study him, his long, lean, sturdy body, the way he caressed the brush. After a while, he turned, and I could see his profile. The sun's rays lit a most attractive face framed by soft, curly brown hair, and when he noticed he had company and looked at me full on, the most dazzling smile and kind, deep blue eyes I'd ever seen.

It had started out as an ordinary day. One look at the stranger and nothing was the same again. One look was not enough, would never be enough. I almost dropped my basket of eggs. The man's mouth was open wide, and he wouldn't stop staring at me. But I didn't think he was rude. I thought he must like what he saw. I see the way men look at me, at church, at the farmer's market, even at home, on the mountainside. But this man was different. He didn't look at me with lust in his eyes but with wonder, like he couldn't believe I was real and alive on this earth and standing right in front of him.

It was bold of me, but I walked right up to him and held out my hand.

"I'm Bernice, Bernice Brady, but everyone calls me Necey. I've never seen you around here before."

He managed to close his mouth when he took my hand in his. It was like a lightning spark, the kind of instant attraction you read about in romance novels. His hand felt warm in mine. I didn't want to let it go, and by the silly grin on his face, neither did he.

"I'm Moss. Moss Hathaway." He waited a beat, like he expected me to recognize his name, and when I didn't, he nodded toward his easel. "I'm a painter."

I studied the canvas. This was no ordinary artist. "Your work is beautiful. Have you come to Confrontation to paint our mountain?"

Moss continued to hold my hand, so I had to steady the basket on my other arm.

"My car broke down at the bottom of the mountain, and the Rushings were nice enough to let me stay with them for a while. They won't take my money, so I'm doing a painting of their cabin as a gift."

"How long's a while?" I asked, hoping I didn't sound too eager.

He swung my hand and circled his finger lightly across my palm, creating another electric shock.

"Well, now, Miss Bernice-Brady-everyone-calls-me-Necey"—and he smiled when he said my name—

"that depends on how long the Rushings can tolerate me and whether you'll be around."

The man made me laugh, so right away I knew he was someone I wanted to get to know.

"I live just across the way. I bring fresh eggs to the Rushings every morning."

I shifted the basket again because my arm was going numb. I couldn't stop staring at him. The painter took the basket from my arm and offered to take it inside to the Rushings.

"I'm new here, and I could really use someone to show me around, point out the best scenes from daily life in a small town, the most unique spots for me to paint."

And that's how it started, our daily excursions around the mountain, our precious picnics in the woods, our secret romance. For the first time in my life, I was in love. I wanted to sing it to the world, shout it out to the mountain, but I didn't dare breathe a word to my sisters, in fear that my brother or father would find out. Stolen moments in seclusion were all we had, but it was enough, at first. And there were the letters, the precious love letters from Moss, that I read and reread every night, every minute we were apart.

~*~

My love,

I can hardly wait until daylight, when I can see you again, touch you again. Tell you how I feel. Show you what's in my heart. My hands are yearning to paint you. I can see you in my sleep. I can feel you near me. Before I met you, my life was dark. I wanted to run away from the world and now you are my world. I'm ready to face anything with you beside me. When my eyes fell upon you, suddenly the fog lifted. Out of the mists, the world shifted into focus in a riot of color. The vision of loveliness that you are lights up my existence. The sky seems bluer, the colors brighter, the mountains higher, the air sweeter. All the corny phrases that lovers spout don't seem so trite.

Your devoted admirer, Moss

Moss

I made a promise to myself. The next time I see Necey—the next time I can truly breathe—I will tell her the truth. That I am a married man, but that my marriage no longer brings me joy, peace, or contentment. That I could no longer work, that I had lost my way until I came to Confrontation. My wife, who seems no happier in our marriage than I am, has asked me for a divorce. We talked about it before I left. She admitted she finds me strange. She used to be attracted by my talent, but now she is jealous of all the time I spend away from her creating, traveling to distant places to find inspiration. She wonders why I can't find inspiration at home, with her. I tell her I'm a landscape painter and landscape painters paint landscapes. So, naturally, I have to travel to find scenes I want to paint. She no longer wants to share my bed or my life. She says she has found love with another man, a man whose head isn't in the clouds, who is always around for her, and she wants to start a new life with him. Whatever love we once shared is squandered with rash words and recrimination. I had to leave, and in leaving I found a love like I have never known before.

I knew it the moment I laid eyes on her. I've heard that love at first sight is like a lightning strike, but I never believed it could happen that way. But when I saw Necey, in all her perfection, I fell under her spell. It wasn't just her looks, although she looked like she had stepped out of a Botticelli masterpiece, a Venus for the ages. She had a smile that would put Mona Lisa to shame. Her soul spoke to mine. I couldn't wait to get back to my paints to try to capture both her inner and outer beauty. But I doubted I could do her justice.

And when I picked up my brushes and put them to canvas, it was as if I were possessed. How to capture that waterfall of hair, the way the light played on it, spinning it to gold. The curve of her perfect cheek, the barest hint of breast, the eyes—Oh, God, the eyes that seemed to look right through me. Her lips were perfection. And I wanted those lips on mine. There were no longer any limits. I was a landscape painter who couldn't stop painting portraits of the woman he loved. What would the art world make of that? To tell you the truth, I didn't care.

****

Amelia put the letters down on the coffee table. The heat generated by the words was almost combustible. She wanted to get back to them, but as they grew more intimate, the picture they painted was one of forbidden love, an inevitable dance that could have only one outcome. She felt like an intruder, but she couldn't turn away. She was compelled to keep reading. The fact that the words were written by Moss Hathaway made her even more anxious to get back to them.

****

Necey,

At last, we're alone. The Rushings are on an outing, one I fear they invented for our benefit.

"We'll be away most of the day, Moss, so feel free

to make yourself at home. Take whatever you need." I wonder if they know that what I need, the only thing I need, is you, my darling Necey. I think we may be more transparent than we think. How could we not be, when we're a couple in love? When I walked up to rearrange your drape, my hand accidentally touched your breast, and you exploded into my arms. Your nipples stood erect, protruding from that diaphanous robe, longing for my touch, and I fell on you or you fell on me. I don't know who made the first move, but I could no longer contain my passion. We were both ready. I lifted you from the floor and carried you into my bedroom. And I let my wildest fantasies play out. I touched those rosy pink tips and licked them and drank from them and touched your body all over. You were so wild for me, my darling, and you exceeded my fantasies of our coming together.

When I learned of your virginity, I could hardly control my need. I moved ever so slowly at first, but you bucked beneath me and wouldn't let me linger. You wanted me inside of you, and there was no other place I wanted to be. You were eager to learn, and I was eager to teach you, to make you mine in every way.

I saw the bruises and I didn't ask questions, just kissed them and kissed you, my darling, in all your sensitive parts, and you gave yourself to me so sweetly my heart wanted to break. I wanted to keep you safe beside me forever.

Will I ever know all your secrets? Mrs. Rushing told me your father and brother keep you locked away from the world, away from potential suitors, away from life, in a proprietary, unnatural way. I can see you have suffered, but you gave yourself to me without hesitation, bursting with love, moving under me, filling me, completing me in a way I've never been loved before. You taught me more about love that one morning than I could ever teach you in a lifetime. You are mine. I am yours. I would lay down my life for you.

Yours forever, Moss

~*~

My darling Moss,

I never knew love could be like this. When you touch me my body sings. I want to be with you every minute of every day. I can't stand to pose because when I look at you, at your beautiful face and your strong body, I can only think of one thing. I fear I am jealous of your talent. I want to throw away your paints and brushes so you can focus only on me. I want to lay with you, warmth against warmth, your body against mine. I want you inside me. If that makes me a wanton woman, then I am guilty. You are my master. I am your slave. I am your master, you are my slave. There is no me. There is no you. There is now only us. There is nothing I wouldn't do for you. I never knew what I was meant for until you released me. I will come to you, every morning, every night, every moment, so I can be in your arms, no matter the consequences. I can never get enough of you, my darling. No one can keep me from you, my love. There is a whole wide world out there, and I want you to show it to me. We will run away from this place and I will be yours, always and forever.

Your Necey

Necey

"If I tell you a secret, will you promise not to tell Pa or Bundy, especially not Bundy?"

Barbara and Brenna locked pinkie fingers. "Pinkie swear," they announced at the same time, chanting the verse they used to sing growing up when they said the same thing at the same time.

Barbara: "What goes in the oven?"

Brenna: "Bread."

Barbara: "What goes up the chimney?"

Brenna: "Smoke."

Barbara and Brenna: "May your wish and my wish both come true."

"Now you have to tell," coaxed Barbara.

Necey fairly vibrated with excitement. Barbara and Brenna gathered around their sister on the front porch swing. When she had their rapt attention, she began.

"I'm in love."

"Don't stop there!" Barbara exclaimed.

"Tell us everything," Brenna insisted. "Who is he? And how did you find him?"

That was the biggest mystery of all. Men, at least men who weren't related to the Brady family, were a scarce commodity in Confrontation. When a woman was marrying age, a man from the neighboring town was usually found to fit the bill. No one ever left Confrontation. Few were allowed to breach the "inner circle," the Brady inner circle.

Necey kneaded her hands together. "It's the stranger across the road."

"The handsome stranger?" Brenna's eyes grew wide.

"The painter over at the Rushings?" Barbara asked.

"His name is Moss. Moss Hathaway."

"Moss, like the fur that grows on the Bald Cypress?" Brenna and Barbara both laughed.

"Not Spanish Moss. Moss is his given name."

"We didn't even know you knew him," said Brenna. "How did you meet?"

"I was delivering eggs to the Rushings about three months ago when I saw him outside, painting," explained Necey. "We started talking, and he asked me to help him find locations he could paint, and one thing led to another, and…"

"It was love at first sight," Barbara teased.

"It was. We're in love. Really in love."

"You're serious," Brenna said.

"Yes, and we're going to run away together tomorrow morning. I just finished packing. I wanted to say goodbye. I even borrowed Mama's wedding dress, although she doesn't know it. We're going to get married right after his divorce comes through."

"His divorce!" The girls spoke at once. "He's married?"

"Yes, but he's working things out with his lawyer. He gave me this ring." Necey thrust out her left hand to flash the emerald-and-diamond ring in front of her sisters.

"That ring could blind a person," Brenna said, clutching her sister's ring finger.

Barbara reached out and admired the stone. "It's beautiful, Necey."

"Thank you. I just wanted you to know that his intentions where I'm concerned are serious."

"When were you planning to break the news to Bunnell?" Brenna inquired.

Necey paled. "Never. If I tell Bunnell, he won't let me leave. You know that."

"Darn right," agreed Brenna. "He'd tie you to a post, and then he'd go after Moss with a shotgun."

"That's why you've got to swear not to tell him," Necey pleaded. "Don't make me sorry I told you."

"Necey, our brother's got eyes and ears everywhere. He'll sniff you out, and when he does, he'll never let you go. He'll probably beat you, too."

"He'll do more than that to you," Brenna warned. "He'll do what he's been itching to do ever since you started blossoming into a woman."

Necey shrank back and declared, "That is never going to happen. He's my brother!"

"When our brother gets riled, anything can happen," Barbara said. "And this time, we won't be able to stop him. It's you he wants. It's you he's always wanted. And he's ashamed of it, too, which makes it worse. Which is why he's always punishing you for something you can't even help. He's been fighting it, but for all his talk about good Christian values, he's lusting after his own sister in his heart. But if he can't have you, he'll make sure no one else can."

"Daddy always said you were his brightest star, the sister who got all the looks and the brains," said Brenna. "And Bunnell always said no man was ever good enough for Necey."

"But we're triplets. We look alike."

"But like Daddy said, 'The light went out after they made you.' And Bunnell's been mooning over you ever since. Nursing his secret dream of saving you for his own."

"I love Bunnell like a brother, but not that way," said Necey. "And, he's not *really* our brother, not by blood. It's no big secret Bunnell was left in a bundle on the church doorstep by a madwoman, and Mama and Daddy took him in. And he'd like to kill anyone who says he isn't a true Brady. In fact, he probably has. He's their little angel, sent by God when they couldn't have children of their own. Then, after Bunnell came, she couldn't stop having them."

"I still remember that night Daddy kept calling Mama and tried to sweet talk her into coming to bed and she threatened to hit him over the head with the iron skillet if he came near her again," Barbara recalled. "She always said an iron skillet was the best form of birth control."

"Nine kids are enough," Barbara and Brenna shouted, imitating their mother, before they burst out laughing.

"You all know that's wrong, don't you? I don't want to live my life in fear. I'm going to leave Confrontation, maybe for good."

"We're never going to see you again?" Suddenly alarmed, Brenna and Barbara embraced Necey.

"I'm sure I'll be back. We're going to travel in Europe and live in Italy while Moss paints."

"He make any money on those paintings of his?" Brenna asked.

"He's a famous artist. His work is hanging in

museums."

"Museums? Really?" Barbara acted like she didn't believe her. A museum was a foreign concept to the women of Confrontation. None of the girls had ever visited one.

"Yes, and private collections around the world."

"What about us?" Barbara asked, her face falling into a pout. "What do we have to look forward to? When Bunnell thinks we're ripe for mating, he'll go over to the next town and find us what he calls "two proper men who love the Lord" to breed with. We'll have no choice in the matter. It won't matter if they're as evil as Lucifer or as ugly as sin."

"Or fat as a pig," quipped Brenna. "Love won't have anything to do with it! And don't think Bunnell won't get something out of it. Sometimes I hate that man. "

"How are you going to know what to do without Daddy or Bunnell barking orders at you all the time?" Barbara wanted to know.

"You know that's not the way it's supposed to be. Moss taught me that."

"What else did he teach you?" the girls giggled, and Necey blushed.

"Life with Moss is not going to be like that. I'm going to be my own person. Moss would never raise his voice or raise a hand against me."

"You always did believe in fairy tales, Necey," Barbara said. "We only wish the best for the future Mrs. Hathaway."

"And I want you girls to stick up for yourselves. Don't let Bundy control your lives."

"What should we do next time Bunnell tells us to

fetch him a beer?" Brenna posed. "Should we say, 'Fetch it yourself, Bundy?' "

This time all three girls burst into gales of laughter at the absurdity of that occurrence.

"Baby steps," counseled Necey.

Barbara glanced at Necey and squinted. "You gonna go to your man dressed like that? Those clothes look like they're strangling you, honey, they're so tight. You've been putting on some weight, Necey. I'll loan you one of my dresses that fits—"

Barbara and Brenna focused on their sister like a laser and their mouths fell open simultaneously. Barbara spoke first.

"Bernice Brady! That's not the only secret you've been keeping. Bunnell is going to have your hide. He's really going to punish you this time."

"Lord help us all," Brenna wailed.

Necey rocketed up from the porch swing and rounded on her sisters.

"Don't you dare breathe a word to Bunnell. Moss doesn't even know yet."

~*~

Necey,

Has it only been three months since I first saw you? I feel I have known you forever. When you lie in my arms, I think only of you. I trace my fingers along your neck, over your beautiful breasts, your stomach, and I see a blossoming under my touch. Necey, could it be, could my dream of having a child be happening? I have grown to know every inch of your body, and I detect a change. A sweet secret that you are not ready to share. Perhaps you are not even aware of it. When you are not with me, I paint feverishly, so that when we are together we can be alone, with no interruptions, flesh to flesh, soul to soul. My paintings are the best I have ever created. And that is because you're my inspiration, darling. More and more I am driven to produce, to paint like there's no tomorrow.

The Rushings seem to be eager sightseers. They manage to find the most remote spots in the county to explore. One day it's gem mining—panning for rubies, sapphires, emeralds, and gold. The next it's rafting down the Nantahala. They hardly spend any time in their cabin.

When your father and brother beat down the door looking for their chick this morning, and we didn't answer because we were cocooned in our love nest, they were furious.

And we are deliriously happy. Laughing silently, because we have each other. When we're together, no problem is insurmountable.

And no one can hurt us. It is us against the world, my sweet, innocent Necey.

And I wait for the wonderful news I know you are eager to share, my darling, my only love, Necey. Put me out of my misery and tell me now.

Your soul mate, Moss

~*~

Moss, darling,

You are an artist, so you are ever observant, and you know my body because it is emblazoned in your mind like a memory that won't fade. And so, my love, you have guessed my secret. We have our miracle.

And I will go away with you. I will pack what little I have and come to you at dawn tomorrow, and we will be together.

My love, I have never been so happy as I am at this moment. We'll spend the rest of our lives as a family. Until tomorrow, my love.

Yours forever, Necey

~*~

Amelia bit her lip. To have a man love you that much was beyond anything she had ever experienced or hoped to experience. That was the last letter in the bundle. She had to call her grandmother to find out what had happened. She needed to know the outcome of that beautiful love story. She needed to know more about Moss Hathaway's past, Necey's secret, and the mystery of the missing man and his paintings. The letters dated back thirty years. Alec was thirty years old. Could he possibly be Moss Hathaway's love child? And, if so, did he know the truth?

Part III

The Disappearance of Moss Hathaway

Chapter Eight

Amelia couldn't wait to get her grandmother on the phone. She couldn't waste time on small talk. She needed to know the truth. Her grandmother's mind was fading slowly. Would she remember something that happened so long ago? This time when she called, her grandmother answered on the first ring.

"Grandma, I found a bundle of Necey's letters in her bedroom, and I read them. Moss talked about his paintings and creating his best work ever. Where are they? I've searched the cabin and can't find any paintings except that large one of Necey on the wall of the living room. There are no records of Moss Hathaway paintings after he disappeared into the woods thirty years ago."

Silence greeted Amelia over the phone. Finally, her grandmother answered.

"It's not something I can talk about right now, sweetheart."

"Well, when can you talk about it? I have to know what you don't seem to want to tell me." Amelia sensed her grandmother's hesitation over the phone.

"Not now. Maybe never. I think sending you there might have been a mistake."

Her grandmother was a stubborn woman, so Amelia knew nothing she said would get her to change her mind. Disappointed, she'd have to try again later.

What was her grandmother afraid of? What secrets wasn't she willing to reveal?

Chapter Nine

Amelia straightened Necey's room, cleaned up the kitchen, dusted the furniture, and waited for Alec on the living room couch. She never knew she could be so domestic. At home, she ordered out. She wasn't much of a cook, wasn't interested in cooking in the least. But she was a houseguest, of sorts, even though the house belonged to her family. She even considered putting a batch of cookies in the oven. At this point she would have done anything to keep busy. She feared she would jump out of her skin if Alec didn't come home soon. She had a lot to tell him and a lot of questions to ask him.

Of course, her eyes drifted right to the painting of Necey. How could they not? She was drawn to the emotion, the mystery, the fragile vulnerability, the beauty, the naughtiness, and the happiness expressed in Necey's face. This picture was more compelling than the Mona Lisa. Necey, too, was hiding a secret. She was pregnant with her lover's child, her *married* lover's child. This was the best Moss Hathaway painting Amelia had ever seen.

Her mother had named her Amelia after Amelia Earhart, another famous person who had disappeared. And now she was determined to find the key to Moss Hathaway's disappearance.

Amelia heard a car pull up the steep driveway and

listened as the tires crunched against the gravel. Someone needed to pave that road. She jumped up from the couch and peeked out the window. It was Alec. Her breath caught in her throat. Was she ready to have this conversation?

"Honey, I'm home," said Alec, smiling as he lumbered into the cabin. Well, they both called it the cabin, but it was hardly that anymore. Alec looked like he wanted to scoop her up in a giant bear hug, and she wanted him to, but not now. Getting cozy with her new roommate was constantly on her mind, but now was definitely not the time. Amelia was surprised at how comfortable they already were with each other after only a few days. Her pulse quickened every time she saw him. She couldn't imagine what it would be like to live without him.

Amelia looked up at Necey's picture and for the second time that day wondered what it would be like to have someone love you like that. Specifically, what it would be like to have Alec love her like that. The man was definitely getting to her. She was even developing a soft spot for Confrontation. But now it was time for a confrontation of a different kind.

"Alec," she said, nodding her head and patting a place beside her on the couch. "Come here and sit down."

Alec looked at her strangely. "We need to get going. I have several appointments set up for us."

"The appointments can wait. I need to talk to you."

Alec sat next to her on the couch. "I thought you were all about selling the cabin. Now you're hesitating? Have you changed your mind?"

"I haven't changed my mind, but there's something

we need to discuss first."

"You sound serious. What's this about?"

Amelia pointed to the painting, the focal point in the room.

"It's about your mother. Do you know when this portrait was painted?"

"Sometime before I was born, I guess. She said she was pregnant in the picture, pregnant with me. She said it was the happiest time in her life."

"Yes. But do you know what put that smile on her face?"

"I don't know. My dad, maybe?"

"Who exactly is your dad?" Amelia asked carefully.

Alec's face flushed, and he bowed his head. "I don't know."

"Is it Bunnell?"

"Bundy is my uncle, *not* my father. My mother hated Bundy."

"Are you sure? What did your mother tell you about your father?"

Alec rubbed his arm. "That she loved him so much, and that he would have loved me if he had known me."

"What was the relationship between your mother and Bunnell?" Amelia asked gently.

"She was his sister."

"And nothing more?"

Alec scowled. "It wasn't like that."

Amelia placed her hand on Alec's arm. "Then why don't you tell me what it *was* like?"

Alec pushed her hand away. "You Florida people think you can come up here and dictate morality—your version of morality. You think you can judge us?"

Amelia faced him and spoke deliberately. "That's not what I was trying to do."

"You don't know anything."

"Alec. Who do you think your father was? You must have some idea."

"I told you, I never met my father," Alec said stubbornly.

She risked asking him again. "Do you think your father was Bunnell?"

Alec offered a silent scowl. "Do you know what you're saying? That would be incest."

"Is that why you tolerate him hanging around? Is that why you haven't turned him in to authorities, out of some misguided sense of family loyalty? Is that why you haven't left Confrontation?"

"I thought you came here to sell a house. Now you're snooping into our family business, where you don't belong. You need to go. Now."

"I told you I'm not going anywhere until I sell this house, and now I'm not leaving until I get some answers."

"What kind of answers?"

"The truth. I'm looking for the truth. And I'm not sure you even know it."

Alec raised his voice. "You're not making any sense. You're grilling me. I can smell the smoke a mile away. Everything was fine until you got here and stirred things up. Feelings up."

Amelia bit back a smile. In his way, Alec was admitting his vulnerability to her. He was agitated, but why? She thought he had finally learned to trust her, but that trust was disintegrating.

"Alec, I asked you before if you've ever heard of

the painter Moss Hathaway."

Alec glanced up at the portrait. "His name's on that painting."

"Did you ever wonder why he painted that picture? What his relationship was to your mother?"

"That was a long time ago."

"Alec, did you know that Moss Hathaway disappeared thirty years ago? His car was found abandoned right here in Confrontation. But his body was never found."

"So he got lost. Lots of people do. What does that have to do with my mother?"

"Alec, Moss Hathaway lived in this cabin, and he painted in this cabin, and here is where he fell in love with your mother."

Alec looked stunned. "How do you know that?"

"Wait here," Amelia said, getting up and going to Necey's room to retrieve the packet of letters. She came out and handed them to Alec.

"Here, read these. I believe they're love letters between your mother and your father."

Alec handled the fragile letters as if they were spun of silk, as delicate as orchid blossoms that musn't be touched.

"I never saw these before."

"That's what I thought. Read them, and I'll make us some lunch. It might take you a while."

Alec laid the bundle of letters on his lap and started unwrapping the ribbon, unraveling his past.

Chapter Ten

Amelia sat scrunched up in the rocking chair, under an afghan she had taken from Necey's bed, her eyes focused on Alec, watching his expressions change as Moss's words flowed and his mother's answered. Puzzlement. Amazement. Bewilderment. She wanted to go to him, to comfort him, to fill in the blanks, what blanks she knew, but this was something he had to process himself.

"Do you have a picture of Moss Hathaway?" Alec asked, finally.

"Yes, you can see for yourself. He's all over the Internet." She walked over and sat down next to Alec on the couch. She opened her laptop, and with a few clicks Moss Hathaway stared back at him. The likeness was undeniable. It wasn't just the eyes. It was the entire face. He was staring at the face of his father. A father he never knew. It was apparent Alec hadn't known the truth. That the secret had died with Necey. Had he believed Bundy was his father all this time? He called Bundy his uncle. And who was Marie Antoinette? She called Bundy her daddy. But who was her mother, really? And where was she?

Alec breathed out a strong sigh of relief.

"You can see that it's true," Amelia said gently. "And after reading their letters, how much in love they were."

"But then why? What happened? Why did he leave her if he loved her so much? Why did he leave me?"

"Alec, surely you must have heard stories about a man who came to the cabin and what happened to that man? My grandmother was there that day. She witnessed the whole thing, but she won't tell me."

"What did she say? I want to know exactly what happened."

"Well, I couldn't say for sure, because I wasn't here, but she told me that your uncle came to the cabin and caught Necey and Moss in bed together. He dragged her out of his arms and shoved them both into the living room. But that's as much as she'd tell me."

"Well, then, I need to talk to her. I need answers."

"Of course. I can call her, and we can talk to her together."

Alec fixed his eyes, Moss's eyes, on her. "It sounds like you care what happens to me."

"I need you to sell this cabin for me, so no, I don't want anything to happen to you."

"Is that the only reason? I think I'm starting to grow on you. I think this place is starting to grow on you." It was freaky the way the man could read her mind.

"The truth is I can't wait to get out of here. And I don't know why you stay here. Your mother is gone, so you're free to go back to New York or wherever you want to go."

"What exactly do you have to rush home for?"

"I have a job and a life."

"You told me yourself you don't have anyone to go home to. And this is my home. I'm not selling it."

"It's not yours to sell."

Chapter Eleven

Amelia dialed her grandmother's number and covered the mouthpiece. "Let me talk to her first," she whispered to Alec. "I promise I'll fill you in if she's ready to talk." Alec pounded his fist impatiently into his hand but finally walked into the kitchen to give Amelia some privacy.

Before she could let Alec speak to her grandmother, she needed more information. She needed to solve the mystery of Moss' disappearance.

"Grandma, I need to know what happened that day."

"What day?"

"The last day you saw Moss Hathaway."

Amelia could hear the emotion in her grandmother's voice.

"He shot that beautiful, talented man between his eyes, right in front of all of us."

"Oh, my God, Grandma. You saw Moss Hathaway being murdered?"

"Yes. Necey went crazy, screaming and crying, 'No! No! No!' She ran over to Moss and cradled his head in her arms, and there was blood everywhere on her silky white nightgown. Bunnell was in a blind rage. He turned the gun on Necey, and he would have shot her, too, if your grandfather hadn't intervened.

"Luckily, Bunnell came to his senses in time and

didn't shoot us all. But he threatened that if we ever told anyone what happened, he would kill us. He would hunt us down wherever we were and shoot us. That we could never hide from him. I hated to leave Necey alone with that monster. But she had her sisters and her family. Bunnell got rid of the body, of Moss, and when the police came around, we said nothing. I told Necey she could stay at our place, and we left and never went back. I kept in touch with Necey, and six months later she had a little boy. She said Bunnell never bothered her after the incident, if you know what I mean. Whenever he came around he was always drunk, and when he threatened her she swore she'd go to the police, so he pretty much left her alone. Everyone knew Moss was the boy's father."

So, the whole town of Confrontation had known the truth about Alec's father. Everyone, apparently, but Alec.

"You said he had blue eyes and—" Amelia conjured up Alec's face. There was no doubt in her mind. Alec was the son of Moss Hathaway.

"Does Alec know?" Katherine asked.

"I don't think he did. I don't think his mother told him. She was probably trying to protect him."

"According to her letters to me, they were very close. He took care of her for years before she died. You'd think she would have confided in him. Why don't you ask him?"

"I think he has secretly believed Bunnell Brady is his father. He's ashamed of his uncle, and at the same time he's protecting him out of some misguided sense of family loyalty. Everyone around here knows something, but they're not talking."

"That man shouldn't be allowed to roam free. He was so violent I can't believe he hasn't been locked up by now. Can we be sure your Alec is Moss Hathaway's son?"

"He's not my Alec, but I've seen the pictures of Moss Hathaway, and he's what you'd call the spitting image of his father."

"They were so much in love. And he never got to see his son."

Amelia wiped her eyes, but the tears wouldn't stop flowing. How was she going to break the news to Alec?

Amelia continued to question her grandmother. "Why didn't you report him to the authorities once you got back home?"

"Because I took him at his word when he said he would kill us. He meant it, Amelia."

"I've seen him. He looks like a wild mountain man. He gave me a fright, looking in at me through the picture window the first night I was here."

"You'd better get out of there," Katherine warned. "If that man is still roaming those woods, he's a threat to you if he knows you're related to me. Stay as far away from him as you can. When are you going to talk to Alec?"

"He's in the next room."

"Be careful."

Knowing Bundy had killed Moss, was she brave enough to expose the truth? The last thing she wanted to do was tango with a killer, especially a killer named Bundy. What would she tell Alec? How would she tell him?

If Moss was murdered here, then what happened to his work?

She posed the question to her grandmother.

"Necey gave them to me for safekeeping," said Katherine.

"You've had the Moss Hathaways all these years?" Amelia could hardly contain her excitement. "Where are they?"

"In a safe place."

"Tell me, Grandma, where are they?"

"Are you afraid I'll forget?"

"No, but we can't keep those paintings locked away. They belong in a museum. They belong to the world. Tell me about them."

"There are dozens of them. Unframed, loose, painting after painting. Mostly of Necey, and pictures of the mountains. The cabin. Brilliant pictures. Pictures that would take your breath away. Pictures that would make you swoon."

She couldn't wait to see the rest of the collection. What a discovery! What a treasure trove, and her grandmother had been sitting on it all these years, sitting on one of the biggest secrets of modern times, the solution to the mysterious disappearance of one of the greatest artists of this generation.

"Has anyone else seen them?"

"Over the years, she asked me to sell off a couple of the paintings to help pay for Alec's education. She felt that Moss would have liked knowing that he had contributed to sending his son to college."

"What a sweet thought."

"When I heard that Necey had passed, I thought we should sell the place and be finished with the whole nightmare, which is why I sent you down there. I had no idea Bunnell would still be around after all these years."

"Oh, my God, Grandma. I need to process this. I'll call you back."

Alec came out of the kitchen, a grim look on his face.

"Alec, what's wrong?"

"I was listening in on the other phone." He had overheard the conversation. "Uncle Bundy killed my father?"

Amelia shook her head. "I'm sorry you had to find out that way. According to my grandmother, he did. And my grandparents never returned to the cabin after the incident because he threatened to kill them."

"So Uncle Bundy is not…"

Amelia looked up at Alec. "All the evidence points to the fact that Moss Hathaway was your father."

Alec rubbed his head. "All these years I thought…"

"You thought Bundy was your father." She could see that he had.

Alec paled and then gritted his teeth. "What happened to the body, to my f-father's body?"

"Your uncle buried him. No one knows where, or if they do, they're not talking. Maybe where he buried the bodies of the other people he's killed over the years."

"I need to find my father's grave."

"Why don't we start with Marie Antoinette," Amelia suggested. "I have a feeling she knows more than she's telling. Alec, I never did ask you. Is she really Bundy's daughter?"

Alec shrugged. "All I know is that one day he brought home a pregnant woman to live with him. She gave birth and then, when Marie was just a little girl, she left. So Uncle Bundy raised her. We all assumed she was his."

"It doesn't sound like he's much of a father."

"He stays away. And when he is home he stays drunk and in a sour mood. That's why Marie is here so often. She has no place else to go, no one else to turn to. She has a bastard for a father, if he even is her father. But at least she had a father. Uncle Bundy robbed me of mine. I'm going to track him down and make him tell me what happened, and then I'm going to call the police and have him arrested."

Amelia placed her arm gently on Alec's shoulder. "Alec. Think about this before you go off half-cocked. Your uncle is a dangerous man. I don't think you should confront him like that without any backup. How do you know he won't attack you? Or worse?"

"He won't. He loved my mother, in his way. He wouldn't do anything to me."

"I don't think you should take that chance."

"I need you to go," Alec ordered.

"But, Alec…"

"No, it's too dangerous for you to be here."

Amelia crossed her arms. "I am not going anywhere until this is resolved." The next words out of her mouth surprised her. "I'm not leaving you."

Alec pushed her arm away and reached up for the rifle mounted on the wall. She knew what they were both thinking. That this may have been the weapon Bundy used to kill Moss Hathaway, Alec's father. It was sitting there taunting him.

Amelia tried to stop him, but he maneuvered out of her reach.

"I'm going after him, Amelia. It's the right thing to do."

"Is getting yourself killed the right thing to do?"

"Stay out of my way," he barked, then paused. "Please."

Amelia stepped back and watched Alec stride out of the cabin.

A feeling of unease crept over Amelia. She was beginning to care for Alec, and now she was afraid for his life.

Chapter Twelve

Marie Antoinette and Dr. Landrew walked out of the kitchen. Dr. Landrew had a piece of crispy bacon sticking out of his mouth and a guilty look on his face, if a wolf could look guilty.

Marie Antoinette patted the wolf's head. "Good boy, Dr. Landrew."

Amelia sank onto the couch. "Marie Antoinette, why don't you sit next to me for a minute so we can talk. You can leave Dr. Landrew over there."

"Stay," ordered Marie Antoinette, and the wolf sat obediently on his haunches like a well-trained seal.

Marie Antoinette walked over and glanced sideways at Amelia.

"You don't have to be afraid of Dr. Landrew. He gets along with everybody but Daddy. He don't like the way Daddy smells."

Amelia could understand that. Maybe she and Dr. Landrew could come to an understanding.

Marie Antoinette took a seat beside Amelia. "What do you want to talk about?"

"Alec," she said simply.

"I knew it. You're sweet on him."

"I never said that."

"You didn't have to." Marie Antoinette flashed a smile. "I can see it in your face. Alec is a good man. You couldn't do no better. Them New York girls don't know what they was missing."

"*Those* New York girls don't know what they *were* missing," Amelia corrected.

"Like I said. Cousin Alec's put away money to send me off to college when the time comes. He says it's important for a lady to get an education."

Marie Antoinette primped and folded her hands on her lap to demonstrate her ladylike qualities.

"He's right," began Amelia. Of course her art history degree had done absolutely nothing to help her find employment. But there was no denying it was important to have that degree.

"What did you study in college?" Marie Antoinette asked.

"Art history."

"Then how come you're a realtor?"

Amelia laughed. "That's a good question."

"Alec says a person's got to have marketable skills."

"He's right about that, too." Amelia turned to Marie Antoinette with a serious look.

"Do you know where Uncle Bundy is right now?"

Marie shook her head. "Gone."

"Do you know for how long?"

Marie shrugged her shoulders. "No tellin'. Sometimes he's gone for a week, sometimes months. Sometimes longer. He just picks up and leaves when the feeling comes over him."

"The feeling?"

"The killin' feeling."

Amelia shuddered. The girl couldn't be serious.

"That's just Daddy. He has a temper on him, and when it comes over him he could be dangerous, so he huffs and puffs like a wolf about to blow your house down, and then he goes away to calm down, cool down, and work things out in his mind."

Amelia blew out a breath. By working things out did she mean go on a killing spree? "That couldn't have been easy for you, growing up." She had no idea why she suddenly felt protective toward Marie Antoinette.

"I got Alec and Aunt Necey. Aunt Necey raised me, mostly."

"Your father didn't tell you when he'd be back?"

"Nope," said Marie Antoinette.

Amelia was glad Bundy had disappeared. She didn't want Alec coming anywhere near his uncle. She hoped Alec would be back soon so they could talk, untangle the mystery of Moss Hathaway, figure out what had really happened that day at the cabin.

Amelia hoped he'd stay away for good. But that was too much to hope for. She dreaded the outcome if Alec confronted his uncle about Moss Hathaway. Enough blood had been spilled.

"Marie Antoinette, you mentioned something about a graveyard. Can you take me to it?"

"Sure, me and Dr. Landrew will take you there. C'mon."

Dr. Landrew heard his name being called, and he trotted over to Marie Antoinette.

Marie Antoinette brought Amelia's hand over to ruffle Dr. Landrew's neck. "If you rub his neck like this, he'll know you're his friend. And he'll stop growling at you."

Amelia hesitated, imagining the worst.

"Don't act afraid. He's smart. He'll sense your fear."

Amelia strived to keep her breathing even and pasted on a smile. "Hello, Dr. Landrew. How are you?" she said, talking through her teeth.

"This here's Amelia," said Marie Antoinette. "She's a friend. Pat him again. He likes to be petted."

"Good dog," Amelia said and reached out to smooth Dr. Landrew's neck. The wolf sniffed her private parts and rewarded her with some satisfied sounds. She couldn't believe she was talking to a wolf.

"See, he likes you. Dr. Landrew likes you."

Amelia smiled. She thought Dr. Landrew's owner was beginning to warm to her, too.

"Okay, grab your jacket. It can get cold up at the graveyard."

Amelia put on her jacket and followed Marie Antoinette and Dr. Landrew out the door.

They hiked uphill for what seemed to be miles, although in truth it was probably only a mile. Amelia was out of shape, huffing and puffing all the way, while Marie Antoinette and Dr. Landrew fairly bounded up the mountain. City girls didn't get much occasion to climb mountains and tangle with briars—or bears or wolves, for that matter.

When they finally made it to the clearing, Amelia was faced with a very well-maintained family cemetery surrounded by a freshly painted white picket fence. Marie Antoinette walked over to a gravestone that read, "Here Lies Bernice Brady. Beloved Daughter, Mother and Sister."

"This here's Aunt Necey's grave," Marie Antoinette said. "Cousin Alec puts fresh flowers on his mama's grave every day. Just like she came up here every day to put flowers on the family graves when she was alive. He was devoted to her. He like to fell apart when she died. But he took good care of her. He was a good son."

Amelia's eyes moistened. Alec was almost too good to be true. He was a kind man, a thoughtful man. Somehow, some good had come out of Confrontation.

Amelia noticed that the plot next to Necey's was unmarked. She guessed that was for Alec after he passed. It should have been for Moss, but Moss's body was missing. Who knew what Uncle Bundy had done with him? Maybe he was weighted down at the bottom of a fast-flowing river. If Uncle Bundy was truly a serial killer, somewhere there were pieces of Moss Hathaway buried in a shallow grave or strewn about at the top of a mountain to be dragged away by wild animals. There were numerous ways to dispose of a body. And, according to rumor, Uncle Bundy had plenty of practice in that area.

"What was your daddy's reaction when your aunt passed away?"

"He went on a bender. He disappeared for weeks. Then one day I found him crying on her grave, and I said, 'Daddy, Aunt Necey's gone. It's time to go home.' He was quiet after that, for a while. He has a temper like a thundercloud."

Amelia avoided thunderclouds wherever possible. Thunderstorms reduced her to an almost catatonic state. She looked up and shielded her eyes from the sun. No sign of bad weather on the horizon.

Amelia looked out over the sea of Brady and Randall tombstones. The Randalls must have been the original family before Alec's grandfather came here from New York. The family had lived on this mountain for generations. It was their mountain, and her grandparents were probably looked upon as intruders, the Florida people who bought the land but never really fit into the community. And now she felt like an interloper, even though the cabin was legitimately her grandmother's property. But that was only money. Contracts meant nothing up here on the mountain. The Bradys were akin to God. They were not to be crossed. Katherine Rushing and Necey Brady had shared a history, a dark secret, and because of it, her grandmother had ostensibly been banned from Confrontation. The sooner she sold the land and got out of Confrontation, the better.

But for some reason she was hesitating. That reason was Alec. She'd grown to care for him in the short time she had been here. And it wasn't just his rugged good looks she was attracted to. It was his mind and his caring heart. She wished he could care for her, too. She wondered what it would be like to kiss him.

Someone tapped her on the shoulder.

She jumped up in alarm.

"It's only me." Alec laughed. "You were lost in thought. You must have been daydreaming." Placing his rifle on the ground, he asked, "Thinking about me?" He smiled broadly.

Amelia colored.

"You were, weren't you?"

Amelia dusted herself off. "I most certainly was not."

Alec took her by the shoulders. "Have you ever been kissed in a graveyard?"

Amelia felt lightheaded.

Alec lowered his mouth, his sexy mouth, a mouth

she'd been dreaming about, or at least daydreaming about only minutes before, and placed his lips softly on hers. It was warm, like the sun, and gentle like a caress, and it was like coming home. She wanted more.

When she responded, Alec took it as an invitation and crushed her to him like a starving man, like a man who hadn't been kissed in a long while. She answered his hungry kiss with equal fervor, winding her arms around his neck and bringing him closer until their bodies touched.

"Marie Antoinette?" she whispered breathlessly.

"I sent her home. We're all alone up here."

"And Bundy?"

Alec's face clouded over. "He's gone, for now."

Amelia looked into his eyes. His skewered hers with a question. And when she nodded they fell to the ground, panting, hands and lips entangled. Alec trailed kisses down her face and neck and took off her jacket and tore off her blouse. He unhooked her bra and took her breasts in his hands.

"I've been waiting a long time to taste you, Amelia Rushing. And I know you're going to feel so good."

Amelia's breath hitched as he lifted her butt and pulled off her jeans, pushed her panties down around her knees.

Amelia lifted Alec's shirt over his head and positioned herself beneath him. He managed to discard his jeans, and then they were lying body to body, naked except for their underwear. Kissing, panting, touching everywhere, tongues greedy, testing, tasting, taking.

When Alec pulled off her panties, his fingers began exploring and doing glorious things to her body. He seemed pleased to find her moist and ready. She reached in and touched him, and he was already hard. He pulled down his underwear and lowered his body onto hers.

"I want you, Amelia. Are you sure about this? Because if you are, this is happening."

Amelia nodded. She thought she said, "I'm sure."

"Are you…? I mean…"

Why was he hesitating? Oh, he was asking about protection. He wasn't exactly prepared. Who thought they'd be making love in a graveyard in the middle of the afternoon?

"I'm on the pill," she assured Alec. She'd been on the pill since her breakup with What's-His-Name, never dreaming an opportunity would come up this soon. She was more than ready for Alec. In fact, she thought she'd die if he wasn't inside of her this minute.

"Amelia," he whispered.

"Alec, please, now."

Alec entered her and began a steady rhythm, teasing, then satisfying, swift strokes that were driving her insane. She exploded, and then he came. He clung to her and she to him, and they lay breathless on the holy ground. She thought, just before she passed out from pleasure, this must be what heaven feels like.

"Amelia Rushing, I think I've been waiting for you all my life." And it didn't sound like a come-on or a line. It sounded sincere, like he really meant it. Then, before she slipped off to sleep, he whispered, "I'm never going to let you go."

When they drifted back to consciousness, Alec was sitting up, staring at her, curling his finger around a strand of her hair, humming "She'll be Coming 'Round the Mountain When She Comes."

Amelia's cheeks colored.

Alec kissed her and said, "Did we just do this?"

She nodded.

"Tell me about the men in Amelia Rushing's life."

Amelia sat up and nestled against Alec.

"There aren't any at the moment. There was one, What's-His-Name, but he's off the radar now."

"What was his name?"

"Who?"

"What's-His-Name?"

"I try never to think about him, but his name was Todd." And she realized she hadn't given Todd a second thought since she'd come to Confrontation.

"What about the women in Alec Brady's life?" she asked innocently, not really expecting an answer.

"There were some women who liked me well enough when I was working for a big New York law firm, but a single practitioner in Confrontation, not so much." Amelia could relate, since she hadn't been able to imagine living in this wannabe town.

As Amelia's eyes scanned the sky, she noticed some clouds rolling in. She sat up abruptly and tapped on her iPhone in alarm.

"What's wrong?"

"Don't you see those clouds? The sky is probably going to open up in a minute, and we'll be stuck up here on the mountain. My weather app has detailed radar maps showing where the storms are. Do you see these big green blobs?"

Alec shook his head. "It won't take us but a half hour to walk down."

"Where there are clouds, there's lightning." Amelia struggled into her various pieces of clothing.

Alec laughed but started gathering his own clothes. "Now you're making fun of me."

"They're just clouds. They can't hurt you."

"Let's go. I want to go back to the cabin right now. I don't want to be out here when the rains come. It's not safe."

Alec got up and took Amelia's hands. "We'll leave, then. C'mon. There's nothing to worry about."

"Thank you."

Alec held Amelia's hand as she moved quickly down the dirt path.

"How long have you been afraid of rain?"

"For as long as I can remember. I mean, I don't like to drive in the rain."

"But we're not driving."

"And then gradually I just became worried about extreme weather."

"Hmm."

"We're isolated up here, and on high ground. We'll be the first thing the lightning hits."

Alec pulled her closer. "You're with me. I'm taller than you. The lightning would hit me first. "

"But we're holding hands, so it would hit us both."

"You have an answer for everything, don't you? But I'm attracted to you, even though you are a bit insane."

Amelia smiled. "Take me or leave me."

Alec tightened his hold. "I'll take you, with all your phobias. But if you're going to live on a mountain, you're going to have to get used to the clouds. We're almost in heaven up here."

"Who said anything about living on a mountain?"

"Theoretically speaking," Alec said. "Do you have

any other phobias I should know about? Like commitment phobia?"

"No. But all the men I've dated had that issue."

"I'm not all men. Remember that."

When Amelia started to slip on the gravel, Alec held her up. "Just lean on me. I'll help you down. I'm loyal and trustworthy."

"You sound like a Saint Bernard."

"You could do worse."

"I have done worse. Saint Bernards are rescue dogs, aren't they? I don't need rescuing."

"Nobody's rescuing anyone. I'm just helping you down the mountain, sort of like Heidi and the grandfather."

Amelia studied Alec. He had a good sense of humor. That was important in a man. And he wasn't thrown by her snarkiness. She'd never admit it, but it felt good to lean on someone, and especially good to lean on Alec. He seemed to like her breasts, something What's-His-Name had obviously thought were lacking.

"You're out of shape, honey. We're going to have to do something about that."

Amelia laughed. "Well, there is one more phobia I forgot to mention. I'm afraid of exercise."

Alec dragged Amelia the rest of the way down the mountain. "There are all types of exercise, honey. Like the workout we just got at the cemetery. I think I'm going to put you on a regimen. In fact, I'm going to map out a fitness program that starts and ends in my bedroom."

Minutes later, when they reached the cabin, Amelia bent down, hands on her knees, and tried to catch her breath.

"This mountain is insane."

"I prefer to think of it as majestic," Alec said. "I'm going to make a mountain girl out of you yet."

"I'm only going to be here until I sell the property," Amelia cautioned.

"I have a feeling we're going to run into some serious roadblocks." Alec grabbed her hands and pulled her through the front door. He went into the kitchen and grabbed two bottles of water. He handed one to Amelia.

"Because I have a lousy lawyer?" Amelia smiled.

"No, because the pace is slow in Confrontation. I'm going to show you what I mean in a few minutes."

"Not to lose the romantic mood, but I know you're concerned about finding your Uncle Bundy. Where do you think he is?"

Alec's mood turned sullen. "He's hightailed it out of here, done his usual disappearing act. I don't know when he's coming back or where his hidey hole is, but I'm going to do some investigating while he's gone and get to the bottom of this, and I will confront him when he returns."

Amelia noticed that the rifle was back in its place near the fireplace mantel.

"Shouldn't you get the law involved? I think going after him yourself could be dangerous."

"The law isn't going to do anything to Uncle Bundy. How do you think he's avoided prosecution for this long? He's related to everyone in the county police department. They're protecting him."

Alec took a drink of water. "Amelia, I want to learn as much as I can about my…about Moss Hathaway. Will you help me?"

"Of course."

She caught a twinkle in Alec's eyes.

"But first, I think we need to start your personal training course. Why don't we take this discussion into the bedroom?"

Amelia started toward Alec's mother's room.

He pulled her back. "My bedroom. You're moving in with me."

"You're pretty bossy, aren't you?"

"You have no idea." Alec pulled her up against him and kissed her long and hard before he frog-walked her into his bedroom, slamming the door with his foot. Lifting her up, he placed her on his bed. He moved on top of her, kissed her lips, and began nuzzling her neck.

"When does my lesson begin?" Amelia asked.

"Right now, sweetheart. Pay attention."

Chapter Thirteen

"Now follow my lead," Alec instructed. "Whatever I say, don't disagree with me."

Amelia shrugged. "Okay, we'll play it your way."

They walked up the path to a cottage across the gravel road that ran next to the Rushing cabin. Goldilocks and the three bears lived in a cottage, for goodness' sake. Alec knocked on the door, which was promptly opened by a woman who flashed a welcoming smile.

"Aunt Brenna, I'd like you to meet Amelia Rushing, the girl I told you about, Katherine Rushing's granddaughter. Do you remember Katherine Rushing? She used to own, I mean, she owns the cabin."

Amelia shook hands with Alec's aunt. "It's nice to meet you."

Aunt Brenna was one of the triplets, Alec's Mom's sister, the neighbor to the south of her grandmother's property. The triplets had been identical, but Alec had said his mother had been the real beauty of the family. It must be strange to look into his mother's face every day when his mother was no longer on this earth. From the portrait of Necey hanging in the cabin, Amelia knew what this woman must have looked like in her prime, but now, even thirty years later, Alec's aunt was still an attractive woman. Her clothes, though clean, were not the latest style, nor was her hair, and why would she need to dress up in Confrontation? There was absolutely nothing going on in this town, if you could even call it that. But being around Brenna made Amelia feel overdressed. Her business suit was all wrong for this place.

"Of course I remember her. Alec, your new girl's a beauty. I heard you was courtin' her."

Amelia looked at Alec inquisitively. His girl? I mean, they had slept together, more than once now, but his girl? Maybe, in Confrontation, courting had a different meaning.

Alec didn't deny it. She bit her tongue and kept her promise not to disagree with him.

And how had Brenna heard about her? News certainly traveled fast in Confrontation. Probably Marie Antoinette had mentioned it. She hadn't really met anyone else in the town.

"Now what can I do for you?"

"Amelia is here to sell the Rushing cabin, but before she can do that she needs to get an easement to cross your land to the part of the property that borders yours."

Brenna got a wistful look on her face and addressed Amelia. "You know, I asked your grandparents many years ago if they could grant us an easement to my one-acre tract between the Rushing property and the public road in exchange for our easement, and your grandfather wouldn't allow it."

"That doesn't surprise me," Amelia answered. "Grandpa was pretty stubborn, and he might not have understood the implications of his actions. He probably thought granting an easement would have somehow compromised his property. But he was also very generous. He let the whole town use the spring on his property for their water supply, and he let your family inhabit the cabin for thirty years without compensation."

Brenna nodded. "You sure your girl's not a lawyer, Alec? She uses a lot of fancy words. But this problem could have been solved all those years ago if we could have swapped easements."

"Aunt Brenna, the past is the past. We have an opportunity to set things right. Amelia's grandfather has passed on, and now her grandmother wants to sell the property. You can help make that happen. I walked the location of the easement, and everything seems to be in order. When I write up the sale, I'll include your easement in the agreement, in case you ever want to sell your land."

"I ain't never going to sell this land, Alec."

"I know you won't, Aunt Brenna, but I also know you want to do the right thing."

Brenna crossed her arms and stared at Amelia.

"Well, I trust you, Alec, and since she's going to be in the family and all…"

Amelia turned to Alec and opened her mouth to protest, but he signaled her to be quiet.

"Do you want to sell this property or don't you?" he whispered urgently.

Amelia pursed her lips and nodded her head.

"Well, okay, then, boy, you can write up your paperwork, her easement for my easement. But I'm warning you, there are two more owners between the Rushing property and the public road. The other owners aren't going to be so easy to deal with. When's the weddin'?"

Amelia's jaw dropped, and Alec grabbed her and planted a kiss on her lips to keep her from speaking. "My bride-to-be and I haven't settled on a date yet, Aunt Brenna, but you'll be the first to know when we do. Amelia, let's go. We have an appointment on the other side of the mountain, with an adjacent property owner."

"Th-thank you, Brenna."

"You can call me Aunt Brenna, seeing as you're going to be family."

"Bye, Aunt Brenna," Alec said, steering Amelia away, back toward the cabin. Then Alec turned again to his aunt. "Oh, and I'll be back to fix your plumbing problem later today, and I'll send over one of the cousins to mow your lawn since I'll be tied up with Miss Rushing for a while."

Amelia blushed, imagining herself tied up in bed with Alec Brady.

"Thank you. And if you could bring those groceries I asked you to pick up, I sure would appreciate it. And your Aunt Barbara would like you to stop by to check out a leak in her house."

"Of course. By the way, do you know when Uncle Bundy is coming back?"

Aunt Brenna rolled her eyes. "That ne'er-do-well brother of mine can stay away forever. He's a troublemaker and worse."

"You let me know when he gets back. I've got to talk to him."

"I'm sure the whole mountain will be buzzing when he gets back. Everything is quiet when he's gone, and then it kicks up like a hornet's nest when he returns."

Alec waved.

Amelia waited until they were out of earshot of Aunt Brenna. "Do you take care of all of your relatives?"

"The ones who can't take care of themselves."

"I assume you provide free legal services for your entire family."

Alec's sheepish grin gave him away.

Amelia nodded. "Then how do you make any money?"

"Money isn't the most important thing in life."

"I disagree. If you don't have any money, it's pretty darn important." She thought of her rapidly dwindling bank account and how, if she didn't make this sale, she would have to dip into the parental well, something she'd promised herself she'd never do again. If she had money, she could put a down payment on a house or buy an apartment instead of living with her parents. How irresponsible did that make her? Then there was the matter of the broken engagement and all the expenses her parents had incurred when she'd canceled the wedding. She needed to move forward financially and emotionally.

Alec, on the other hand, had taken on the entire Brady clan as his personal responsibility. He was uber dependable. He was a nurturer. By all accounts, he was quite an amazing guy. He had probably been an Eagle Scout, if they had Eagle Scouts in Confrontation. But he also took liberties with the truth.

"You lied to your aunt," Amelia accused. "You practically have us married off. Don't I get a say in this?"

"I didn't lie. I intend to marry you. I was just a

little premature."

Amelia fumed. "I feel like I'm back in the Stone Age, where the women were just clubbed over the head and dragged off to the caveman's lair."

"You wanted to sell your property, and this was the only way my aunt was going to grant you that easement. And, about the matter of the engagement, my mind is made up. We got Aunt Brenna to say yes, and now all I have to do is get you to do the same."

"Alec Brady, you're impossible. A few days ago I didn't even know you, and now you're planning our wedding?"

"I know what I want. And I don't see as I had much choice. The pickings are pretty slim around here, unless I want to marry one of my cousins."

"So you pick the first girl who happens along?"

"The first *amazingly beautiful* girl," Alec corrected.

"You know this is crazy."

"I know I'm crazy about you." Alec opened the passenger door of his Volvo XC-90 and handed Amelia into the SUV.

The crazy thing was that she half hoped he was serious. But, like he said, it was just a ploy to help sell the land.

"Our next stop is the widow who lives on the other side of the mountain. She probably has the easiest access to your property, according to the mapping system. Her husband always wanted to buy your grandmother's property. Combining the two properties would make a pretty package, and it was his dream to own the top of a mountain. But he passed away while logging on the property, and I don't know the widow's heart in the matter. But if she bought your grandmother's property, her land would be more valuable, so I'm proposing she grant you an easement and then buy your property. If you don't get her approval, any future contract you make for the purchase will be terminated, since the property cannot be sold or even listed by a realtor because it's landlocked. And if she doesn't agree to grant or sell you an easement, the property has little or no value. So you may have to offer her money to purchase an easement that would provide access to her property via the road she owns. This easement will facilitate the sale. If she balks, you could offer to sell her the tract at a discounted rate from the tax-appraised value in consideration of the right-of-way/easement issue. If all else fails, you could approach her widow to widow, from your grandmother's perspective."

"You have it all figured out, don't you?"

"Not at all. Even if this works out, we have to deal with the next adjacent property owner, and he's mean as a buzzard. His property butts up against Uncle Bunnell's land, and he's fiercely protective of it. Your property has access to Brady Cove Road, which is a private road and would require agreement from the owners of that road. So whatever we negotiate with Mrs. Jenkins can't be finalized until we deal with the third property owner. But let me present the offer to her, and you can chime in where you want."

"But if we sold the property, where would you live?"

Alec shrugged. "I'd find a place up around here somewhere."

"You're determined to stay here?"

"It's my home, Amelia."

Amelia didn't like the idea of putting Alec out of the only home he'd ever known. But she had come here to sell her grandmother's property. She couldn't let her personal feelings stand in the way.

They arrived at the widow's house. It was a large, modern-looking house, very picturesque, with a jaw-dropping view. Alec knocked on the door, and when the owner came out, Alec made the introductions.

"Mrs. Jenkins, I'd like you to meet Miss Amelia Rushing. She is Katherine Rushing's granddaughter, and since her husband passed, Mrs. Rushing is interested in selling the property."

"Come in and have some lemonade and fresh-baked cookies," Mrs. Jenkins offered. "I don't get many visitors up this way, and since my husband died, well, it's pretty lonely."

Alec and Amelia followed her into the house. She seated them at a beautiful oak table, poured them each a glass of fresh lemonade, and brought out a platter of peanut butter cookies. It was apparent Mrs. Jenkins had money. Her home was spectacular and beautifully furnished.

Mrs. Jenkins sat down across from them.

"Alec, I was sorry to hear about your mother."

"Thank you, Mrs. Jenkins. I sure do miss her a lot."

"I miss my husband terribly. We had so many plans. He retired, and then he didn't live out the year. Now, why is it you've come to see me?"

Alec outlined the situation and the alternatives.

"So even if you're not interested in permanently owning the property, you could purchase it and repackage part or all of it to sell together with a small portion of your existing parcels to the left and north of the Rushing property, to configure a tract that has access to the county-maintained road," Alec concluded. "I expect you could market the repackaged property at a price significantly greater than the price for which we would be selling the Rushing tract to you."

"Mack sure would have jumped at the chance to buy the Rushing property. That was his dream. I know we talked about it. Just this morning I tried to walk up to the top of the mountain. I can see why my husband wanted to buy that property. The roughed-in road is very overgrown, and with the downed trees, I couldn't get all the way up there, but I am interested in purchasing the tract, if we can agree on a price. Today was the first day it has been nice enough to get up there. Mack always expressed an interest in buying the point. I think that is where he wanted to put our house. Thank goodness that didn't happen, because the road maintenance is already expensive enough. My husband did say he would have problems accessing the lower portion of the property due to the terrain."

"We would be willing to compensate you for that," Alec pointed out.

"I don't need the money, but I would like Mack to have his dream, to own the entire mountaintop. I feel close to him up there. I think he would have liked that. What do I have to do to purchase the property?" Mrs. Jenkins named a price, a much lower price than Amelia had expected, depending on a final clear title search.

"My grandmother will agree to your offer price, with the condition that you pay for one hundred percent of the closing costs and fees."

"That's acceptable. I do not intend to do a survey,

since this will just be added to my tract. With my husband gone, I have no intent to do anything with it."

Alec shook Mrs. Jenkins' hand. "We would be selling the property as is, with no warranty as to access. But if that's agreeable to you, then you can have your attorney prepare the necessary contract/documents for Mrs. Rushing's signature. I'll draw up the papers that verify you will be granting the easement and purchasing the Rushing acreage and bring them back to execute the documents."

Chapter Fourteen

"That was an impressive presentation," Amelia said.

"Thank you, but our next stop is going to be the real test. It may be a deal breaker. I've talked to Mr. Rhinegold, and he is trying to sell his property, too, and expects to have it on the market by the end of next month. He would prefer that the buyer of his property make the decision about whether or not to grant the easement."

"I can't wait until the end of next month. I've got to get back to Florida."

"You may not have a choice. Mr. Rhinegold feels that being at the end of the road gives his property significant value. Like many sellers venturing into this market, he probably overvalues his property. So I fear, but I don't know, that the dollar signs dancing in his head are large enough that he doesn't want to risk the big payout by giving an easement, even for the $3,500 you're willing to offer. My gut feeling is, at this point, you can't offer enough to make it reasonable for you and interesting for him.

"He did say the door was not closed to the easement and that he wants to be a good neighbor, but that is his thinking at the moment. I'm not sure that offering him money right now makes sense, because he believes the real value of his property is its seclusion, which would be disturbed by the easement. Perhaps once his property sits on the market for a while, a little money for an easement will seem more appealing."

"Alec, I can't wait that long. I can't stay here forever. I've got to get back."

Alec hung his head. "You don't like Confrontation, do you? Could you ever see living here?"

"Alec, you've lived in New York. How can you even think that I would be happy living—" Amelia stopped in mid-sentence, realizing she was insulting his home.

"But if you loved somebody, then—well, wouldn't that make a difference?"

How could he talk of love? They'd had sex, great sex, and Alec was a great guy, but love? Could it happen that fast? It had happened that fast for Necey and Moss. But she couldn't leave her home to live on a mountain in the wilderness. She wasn't a pioneer, for God's sake.

"Maybe we can talk about this later," he suggested. "We're here."

Alec and Amelia got out of the car and approached Mr. Rhinegold's cabin. It was remote and stark compared to Mrs. Jenkins' model home. "Secluded" was the word Alec had used. It was definitely that.

Keith Rhinegold was a big man, the size of an ox, and his breath was foul and his body odor reeked. He smelled like he hadn't bathed in weeks.

Amelia wrinkled her nose.

"Mr. Rhinegold." Alec offered his hand. "This is Miss Amelia Rushing." Amelia nodded her head but didn't take his hand. "She's the granddaughter of Katherine Rushing, who owns the Rushing place.

Amelia's grandfather recently passed away, and now Katherine wants to sell the place. In order to do that, they would need an easement from you."

Mr. Rhinegold frowned. "I told you on the phone that this property is special. I'm way up here, the closest place to heaven. What if she sold the property to someone who wanted to build condos on it? It would destroy the natural beauty of the property."

Condos in Confrontation? That prospect was almost laughable. What builder would make an investment like that?

"Well, Miss Rushing obviously can't forecast who would buy the property and what they would use it for."

"I just got married last month. I need to talk it over with the wife, and then I need to have a conversation with God."

Amelia gulped. Somebody married this man? And he had a hotline to God?

"That's fine, Mr. Rhinegold. Just don't take too long. We have some interested buyers, and we might be able to work something out where we don't need your easement. Here's my card. Give me a call when you reach a decision. We'd make it worth your while."

Amelia blew out a breath she hadn't realized she was holding.

Alec put his hand around Amelia's shoulders and guided her to the car.

"That didn't go well, did it?" she asked.

"I didn't expect him to jump at the first offer, but I think he'll come around eventually."

Amelia put on her seatbelt, and Alec started the car and drove back down to the cabin.

It really was beautiful and peaceful here. Could she

ever envision living here? No, not even with a great guy like Alec. What would she do here all day? How could she raise a child here?

Necey had managed it.

Amelia was tired. It had been a long day.

Alec seemed to read her mind. They were growing more and more in tune with each other.

"You sit on the couch and put your feet up on a pillow. I'll massage your feet, and then I'll start dinner. After dinner, we can work on your fitness regimen." He winked at her, pulled off her shoes and socks, and began massaging her sore feet.

It felt glorious. She could definitely get used to this.

"Is it working yet?" Alec asked.

"What?"

"My deadly charm."

Amelia laughed. "I'll admit, this feels good."

"You feel good to me, Amelia. I think we could be good for each other."

"Except for the fact that your hometown is geographically undesirable."

"And I've been to Miami. The traffic is a mess, and there's no change of seasons to speak of."

"But there is a beach."

"If you like to burn to a crisp. Personally, I prefer cooler temperatures."

"Well, then we can agree to disagree."

While Alec was busy cooking dinner in the kitchen, Amelia relaxed. Alec came back into the living room.

"While dinner's cooking, could we do some research on Moss Hathaway?"

"Sure," Amelia said, sitting up. "He was an interesting guy."

"I don't know anything about him, or his art, but I'd like to learn."

Amelia reached for her iPad and motioned for Alec to sit next to her on the couch. She typed in "Moss Hathaway."

Up popped his most recent picture. Alec just stared at it. She'd shown him before, but now that he'd had time to mull over his relationship with the dead artist his interest had increased. Alec was definitely Moss Hathaway's son. They looked just alike.

"It's pretty remarkable, isn't it?" Amelia prompted.

"It's like I'm looking at a picture of myself."

"You're a part of him, Alec." Alec nodded toward the iPad.

"What else is there?"

Amelia scanned the links. "Well, he pretty much disappeared in 1985. His car was found in Confrontation, but not his body. No one suspected foul play. He just disappeared. His wife never heard from him again. The police couldn't find evidence of him. A few of his paintings turned up in private collections over the years, but no new Moss Hathaways have surfaced on the open market since his disappearance."

"Was he a good artist?" Alec asked.

"He was amazing. I studied him in college. Here, let me show you some of his work." She positioned the iPad again into Alec's range of vision.

Alec concentrated on the paintings.

"His work hangs in museums and private collections all over the world," Amelia said. "If a new Moss Hathaway painting was discovered today, it would be worth millions. He has quite a cult following."

"I mostly see landscapes," Alec observed.

"That was his specialty. He traveled around the country capturing the beauty of the land. He has a very realistic style. If he paints a tree, you can tell it's a tree. In a Hathaway, a cloud is a cloud. A lake is a lake. A person is a person, not a jumble of cubes. But the one he painted of your mother was nothing like his original work. It has a lightness about it, a freer use of color, and he had never painted portraits before. Your mother must have really inspired him."

"The letters said he had painted other things here. Your grandmother said she has them. I'd like to see them."

"I'm dying to see them. Would you have time to come to Miami?"

"I can take off for a few days. I doubt we'll hear from anyone about the property immediately. Let's give the buyers a chance to consider our offers. We can fly down there. I'd like to ask your grandmother some more questions about Moss and my mother. She saw them together for the last time."

"Alec, I can't afford to fly down there. And I don't fly during hurricane season."

"The flight is on me. It's something I'm asking you to do, so don't argue with me. And hurricane season is only just beginning."

"Okay. I'm sure she would love to meet you. I'll call her." Alec wandered back into the kitchen.

Amelia picked up her cell phone and dialed her grandmother.

"Grandma, yes, everything's fine. We're getting

close to selling the property. How are you doing?"

"Your father brought me over to Eternal Gardens again. He said we were just stopping by to see if I liked it. But I had to sign some papers. I have all this space here, and in that place I'd only have one room. The bathroom, the kitchen, the living room, the dining room, the bedroom—all in one room. And there's no balcony. How am I going to get my fresh air? "

"Dad said they offered two meals a day, and you could also get lunch if you wanted. Wouldn't that be nice if you didn't have to cook anymore? And I understand they have a nice pool. You could sit outside and read. And they have a piano player every night at dinner. And bingo and an exercise room."

"I hate to exercise. We had dinner there. It was good, but I don't want to live there. I'm not ready for that place. All those people are half gone. Why would I want to be locked up in a place like that?"

"Grandma, you're not being locked up. You'll be living in luxury with all the conveniences. Dad doesn't want you living alone, and you hated having people in the house to help you."

"I told you and I told him, I don't need any help, but I think he's already signed me up. I don't think I have a choice."

"Oh, Grandma, I'm sorry. Listen, I want to fly back to Miami tomorrow, and I'm going to bring Alec Brady with me."

"Oh, that would be lovely. I'll get to meet Moss and Necey's son."

"And Grandma, we want to see the paintings. Can you come with us and show us where they are?"

"Of course. They're in a secure place, and they're

being well preserved. I'm glad you're going to get them so I don't have to worry about them anymore."

"I'm sure Necey appreciated you taking care of them all these years. So we'll see you tomorrow then."

"Bye, sweetheart. I can't wait to see you."

Alec wandered back into the living room and plopped down on a recliner. "Marie Antoinette dropped by while you were on the phone with your grandmother. I gave her permission to stay here while we're gone, and I told her to call me as soon as Uncle Bundy gets back. I've wrapped up everything at the office, so we're clear to go."

Amelia checked her weather app.

"What are you doing?"

"Checking the radar to see if it's okay to fly."

"You know that's crazy, don't you? The airlines aren't going to let a plane take off if it's not safe."

"I don't believe in taking chances."

Alec threw up his arms. "What am I going to do with you? You know your fears are irrational, don't you?"

"Maybe, but they're my fears, and the app says it's okay to go. I'll start packing."

Amelia went into her bedroom and put her remaining clean clothes into a carry-on bag, then checked on Alec. He was throwing some undershirts, cotton briefs, blue jeans, and a couple of dress pants and shirts into a black wheeling bag. He might be a country boy, but he seemed determined to look presentable in front of her grandmother. Country Mouse goes to the Big City.

Amelia could hardly contain her excitement. She would be the first person in decades to see the new

Moss Hathaway collection. Her grandmother hadn't looked at the paintings since she sold the last one to finance Alec's law school expenses. Finally, her art degree would come in handy. The paintings belonged to Alec now, but she could counsel him on how to proceed, help him value the work, connect him with some galleries or dealers or museums when he was ready to dispose of the collection.

She hoped her grandmother had really kept the collection in the right conditions all these years so the paintings hadn't deteriorated. She didn't know what they'd find, but she had never been looking forward to anything more.

Chapter Fifteen

Amelia stepped out of the rental car. She was a bit nervous about her grandmother meeting Alec for the first time. Alec had checked them into a hotel on the beach at Fort Lauderdale, close to her grandmother's condo, and they had deposited their luggage in their room. He'd only reserved one room, which made perfect sense since they would probably be spending the night together anyway. She hadn't objected. In fact, she was eager to be alone with him.

At her grandmother's retirement development they rode the elevator to the fourth floor. They walked to the end of the hall, and she knocked on the door of her grandmother's condo.

When Katherine Rushing came to the door, Amelia threw her arms around her. Then she stepped back.

"What a surprise!"

"Grandma, I told you we were coming. Didn't you write the date down on your calendar?"

"What calendar?"

Amelia winced. Her grandmother was regressing at a rapid pace. She walked over to the dining room table and picked up the calendar. Then she brought it over to her grandmother. "It's right here. Amelia's visit."

"Oh, yes. Now, I remember."

"Grandma, I'd like you to meet Alec Brady. Alec is Necey's son. Alec, this is my grandmother, Katherine

Rushing."

Katherine swayed and placed her hand over her forehead.

Alec caught her in his arms. "Are you feeling okay, Mrs. Rushing? Why don't you have a seat?" He escorted Katherine to the couch.

"I'm sorry. It's just that, for a minute, the years slipped away. You look so much like your father. I thought I'd seen a ghost. I thought Moss had come back."

Alec took the chair across from her, and Amelia sat next to her grandmother after handing her a glass of water. Her grandmother's short-term memory was shot. She only hoped she wouldn't have difficulty remembering or relaying events that took place thirty years ago.

"It's obvious where Amelia gets her good looks."

"This one's a charmer, Amelia." Katherine smiled. "Just like his father."

"I've been telling Amelia that."

"You have no idea how much you favor your father. It's uncanny. Not only your looks but the way you talk, your mannerisms. It's as if Moss himself were sitting in the room with us. I remember him like it was yesterday."

Alec looked across the room and noticed the large painting of the cabin.

"Is that a Moss Hathaway?"

"Yes, it is. Your father gave us that painting so we would always have a bit of the mountains in Fort Lauderdale."

"Tell me about him," Alec prompted.

Katherine took a drink of water and set down the

142

glass on a coaster.

"He was a handsome man. And he was a good man. And he was so much in love with your mother. I've never seen two people more in love. They would have lived a long and happy life together, if—"

"Go on," Alec prompted.

"It still upsets me to talk about that day. If only they had been left alone. They had a brief period of happiness, and for that your mother was grateful. But they were cheated—she was cheated—out of the life they could have had. They had such big plans. They could have had an amazing life."

"I heard you talking to Amelia over the phone. I know what my uncle did, but I want to hear the details from you. Until Amelia told me, I never knew who my father was. My mother never told me."

"That's because everyone was afraid of Bunnell. Everyone knew what had happened. It was such a small community, but it was locked up tight. No one said a word, not to the police, not to you. No one ever mentioned it again because of Bunnell's threats.

"But after I left, Necey called me and wrote to me frequently. I was the only person she could talk to about Moss. She called me when you were born because she knew how excited I'd be that Moss had left a legacy. She was so proud. I don't know how she could have stayed there on that mountain after what happened, but she had nowhere else to go. I let her use our cabin because I was never going back there."

"How did you first meet him, my father?"

"I remember the day like it just happened. Amelia's grandfather and I were in our rocking chairs on the front porch, just about twilight. A man, a very handsome but exhausted man, came walking up the hill and told us he had driven all day and his car had overheated. He asked could he use our phone to call for assistance. Of course, we didn't have a phone back then, but we invited him in, gave him something to drink and a nice meal, and offered him the spare room to stay the night, since it was obvious nothing was going to get done before morning and he couldn't have taken one more step, he was so worn out. I think it was fate that brought your father up that mountain.

"We talked for hours, and he opened up to us. We asked if anyone would be missing him or would be worrying, and he said no. He was married, but his marriage was a source of unhappiness. His wife didn't want children, and she had turned to someone else. He needed to get away. He needed a change of scene. He told us he was an artist. Of course we'd never heard of him. My husband, Will, and I didn't know much about art. But after I saw his paintings, I admired his work tremendously.

"The next morning, Will drove Moss to the bottom of the hill and helped him unload his suitcase and his art supplies. Will took a look at the car and declared it undrivable. By then, Moss was rested and, after looking around the property, asked if he could possibly rent the spare room. He fell in love with the mountain and had to paint it. We could use the money, so we agreed. But then we didn't want to take any money from him. So after a while he painted that picture for us.

"He was outside painting when your mother, when Necey, came around with her basket of fresh eggs for us. One look at her and Moss was head over heels. Necey was shy, but you could tell she was interested in him, too. They were thunderstruck, like you see in the movies. It was like there was a live wire strung between them, and from that moment on they were bound together as one."

Alec smiled and bowed his head. "And then what?" He was as excited as a little boy riding a shiny red bicycle when he asked about his parents' relationship.

"Well, then, he set about painting her," Katherine said. "He told us he hadn't painted in months. He had come to the mountains for inspiration, and he found it when he set eyes on Necey. He couldn't wait to set up his canvases, paints, and brushes. So he painted Necey everywhere—in front of the cabin, up at the cemetery, at the top of the mountain, and by herself. She became his artist's model. For the first time in her life, she was the center of attention. Not one-third of the triplets, not a sister, not a daughter, but a lover. It was her first and, I imagine, her last time in love.

"Moss was living with us, so we tried to give them some privacy. I swear, we must have seen every single attraction in the state, twice, including the casino, and Will wasn't a gambler. We thought we were being subtle, but they could see right through us. The cabin was a safe haven for them.

"And the paintings. Oh, my, they could take your breath away. They were so honest and pure, so real. He told us the three months he was living with us were the most productive time in his career, and, of course, the happiest."

"Where are the paintings now?" Amelia asked.

"At first, I kept them here in the condo so Necey would have easy access to them. But I never heard from Necey after the—incident. Not until you were born. She said she didn't want them anymore, but I think she was just afraid to keep them in Confrontation because of her brother. She was afraid he might burn them. So I rented a temperature-controlled storage unit, and that's where they've been ever since.

"Alec, your mother did instruct me to sell one to help finance law school."

"I wondered how she could afford to send me to Duke," Alec said. "I worked two jobs, but it was way beyond our means. She contributed a lot, but there were a lot of expenses."

"She thought it would be like Moss himself was paying for your education."

"When can we see the paintings?" Amelia asked anxiously.

"We can go right now. The storage unit is not far from here." Katherine got up, picked up her purse and her cane, and led Amelia and Alec to the front door.

"There's more I'd like to ask, like to know," Alec said.

"We can talk more about it when we get back," Katherine said.

Amelia opened the door and looked up at the sky.

"It's a sunny day," Alec said. "Not a cloud in the sky."

"You don't know South Miami. It rains almost every afternoon."

"But you're not driving, so it shouldn't matter," Alec pointed out.

"So you've uncovered my granddaughter's deep dark secret—her weather phobia."

"Yep," Alec said.

"Her grandfather had the same weather issues. It

got worse with age." Katherine locked the door to her condo. "We couldn't plan an outing until he'd checked the weather. Everything we did was weather-dependent. It dictated where we could go and when we could go. Where are you parked?"

Alec pointed out the gray Lexus SUV in the parking lot. He took Katherine's arm and escorted her to the car. She held on to him with one arm and maneuvered on the cane with her other hand.

"And he's a gentleman, too," Katherine said pointedly, looking at Amelia, in case her granddaughter hadn't noticed.

"Yes, he's quite a guy," Amelia agreed, sarcastically. But actually, Alec was that and more. He was the total package, except for the fact that he lived in Godforsaken Confrontation. And the fact that he really didn't want her to sell the cabin, her grandmother's cabin, because he thought of it as *his* home, even though he'd never actually owned it. She had the sense he was just humoring her while at the same time throwing obstacles in her path.

They drove a short distance to the storage facility. A storage unit Amelia had never known about. She wondered whether her father even knew about it. It was a nondescript gray structure. It reminded Amelia of a small prison and, like a prison, it was like a fortress. Her grandmother entered the code on the keypad from a yellowed piece of paper she had in her handbag, and a door rattled open. When it closed behind them, Amelia had an eerie feeling. The long empty hallways were isolated. They were locked in. Anyone might be lurking in the cavernous space.

"Grandma, I hope you don't come here at night or

by yourself."

"I haven't been here in years, not since your father sold my car."

"Does Dad even know about this place?"

"No one does. Except you two, now. Necey swore me to secrecy. I was afraid of Bunnell, and so was she. I'm glad you are here, Alec. The contents of this locker belong to you now. I think it would be a good idea if you took them back with you to Confrontation when you go. Amelia's father is moving me into Eternal Gardens in Miami. It's on the other side of town. I won't be able to get back here. I'd like to close out the locker."

They made slow progress down the hall, the sound of Katherine's cane echoing off the walls, until they got to Unit 555. Katherine took out her key and handed it to Alec. "You have to open it from this lock at the bottom. I can't bend over anymore."

Alec took the key, bent down, and opened the lock, then raised the steel door by hand.

"Grandma, how did you ever manage to access this unit?"

"Well, it was thirty years ago. I was a lot younger then, and in better shape, and I still had your grandfather to help."

"You've been paying rent on this storage unit all these years?" Amelia wondered.

"Necey sent me a check now and then to help cover the cost."

Alec closed the door behind them, and they walked into a large, air-conditioned space.

The paintings were wrapped individually and stacked against each other.

Alec began unwrapping them, one at a time. It was like discovering some long-lost treasure that had been unearthed in a sunken ship.

The first one was a large oil-on-canvas painting of Necey, similar to the one in the cabin. She was nude but tastefully draped, and Alec held his hand to his mouth. Tears streamed out of his eyes.

"Look how young she was."

"Young and beautiful," Katherine added. "The most beautiful girl I've ever seen. He captured her perfectly, her outer beauty and her inner beauty."

"I wish I had known her," Amelia said.

"There are many more like that, of Necey outside, with the mountains in the background, with a basket of fresh eggs. Necey in her element and, in the end, Moss in his." Alec studied a self-portrait. It was as if his father had come alive. He touched each of the canvases reverently, handling the same paper his father had touched, as if he were trying to summon his father's spirit, trying to find some connection. His eyes seemed to hold out hope that, by some miracle, Moss might materialize right in front of him.

"He had so much talent. I didn't inherit that from him. I imagined, I hoped, I might meet my father one day."

Katherine ambled over to the paintings and made a selection. "This is one of my favorites." She pulled the wrapping off, revealing Necey as a laughing wood nymph on the floor of a forest, a waterfall cascading in the background.

"Grandma, these paintings are amazing. The colors are wonderful. This is definitely a new style for him. I'd never seen a Moss Hathaway portrait before the one of

Alec's mother in the cabin."

"Yes, they're remarkable. He was a major talent."

A sealed envelope slipped out of the back of the wood nymph painting. Amelia lifted it from the floor and read the outside words.

"Alec, this is for you. It's from your father, addressed 'To My Son or Daughter.' " She handed it over to Alec, who held it reverently.

He opened it carefully and took his time reading it. Then he handed it back to Amelia.

To My Son or Daughter—

I can't wait to meet you. I don't know whether you'll be a boy or a girl. But that doesn't matter. What matters is that you know how much I love you and your mother. Whoever you turn out to be, you can count yourself lucky to have a mother like Necey.

I want you to grow up and be whatever you want to be, whether that's a painter, a poet, or even the President. I'm sure you'll be smart, like your mother, and sweet. And I hope you take after her in the looks department, because I look more like Abraham Lincoln, tall and gangly. It's a miracle your mother even gave me a second look. But I'm glad she did or you wouldn't be in this world.

I have a lifetime of things to teach you, and I can't wait to start. If I have one lesson to pass on, it's never to give up on love. I hope you find the kind of love your mother and I have had, and when you do, don't ever give it up or give up on it.

Your Proud Dad

Tears streamed down Amelia's face, and she licked them from her mouth. Necey Brady must have been some woman.

"I'd like to hold on to this," Alec said, taking the letter from Amelia.

"Of course."

Then they looked through the rest of the stacks of paintings.

"They're also priceless," Amelia said. "When news of a new collection by Moss Hathaway surfaces, it is going to set the art world on fire. And after all these years, the world will finally know what happened to Moss Hathaway. One of the great mysteries of the last century will be solved. And the greatest gift of all will be the release of these fabulous paintings."

"Amelia, we can't tell anyone what happened. That would mean Uncle Bundy would be tried for murder."

"Alec, he should be. He killed your father."

"You don't understand."

"I guess I don't. Why don't you try to explain it to me?"

"Uncle Bundy has been like a father to me. He's gruff and controlling, and there have always been rumors about missing people and suspicion that he might be responsible, but he was the only father figure I knew. He took care of us, my mother and me. My mother had no way of earning a living. She was dependent on Uncle Bundy. I sensed there was tension between Bunnell and my mother, and maybe fear, but he was always kind to me. He thought of me as his son. For all these years, I thought I *was* his son. I was ashamed, but—"

"But now that you know the truth…"

"What is the truth? What do we really know? I was going to confront him, but he disappeared again."

"You were going to confront him with a shotgun,

as I recall," Amelia put in.

"I was mad."

"You should be. He cheated you out of the life you could have had, should have had."

Katherine placed her hand on Alec's arm. "Why don't we take these paintings to the car, clear out this locker for good. Then we can go back to my condo and talk. I can tell you exactly what happened that morning at the cabin."

Chapter Sixteen

The Moss Hathaway canvases were stacked at attention against the living room wall of Katherine Rushing's condo like obedient soldiers. Alec was slumped in a leather recliner, staring at Amelia and her grandmother, who were seated on the sofa. His posture was an indication of his mood—dark and defeated. He was expecting the worst.

"Are you sure you want to hear this now?" Amelia wondered. "Maybe you'd like to go back to the hotel to rest and relax, and we can talk about this tomorrow."

"No," Alec said. "I've waited thirty years to hear it. I want to know what really happened that morning in the cabin—every detail. I have a right to know."

Katherine clasped her hands on her lap, nodded, and began her story.

"Moss had been with us about three months. It was obvious he and your mother were in love. They couldn't hide it, but they met in secret. They had to because—"

"Because of Uncle Bundy."

"I'm sure you are aware of what a controlling, possessive man he is. He and your grandfather, Necey's father, were cut from the same cloth. I myself was afraid to go near them. I always had a sense they were watching me like feral animals, barely restrained, with their teeth bared, ready to attack when they caught the scent. They terrorized your mother and her sisters. The girls were home schooled. They weren't allowed to date or have any kind of relationship with a man. Your mother was a very smart woman. She was self-taught. She read every book she could get her hands on. But the girls didn't have any kind of freedom."

"He was overprotective." Alec nodded. "He still is."

"To the extreme."

"Did he ever…?"

Katherine knew what the boy was asking: Had Bunnell ever crossed the line with Necey or either of her sisters.

"I can't tell you for sure about your aunts, but he never touched Necey. Oh, he wanted to. You could see it in his eyes. He was hungry for her, but of course she wanted nothing to do with that. She made that clear, but her brother was the type to take what he wanted. She wanted to get away from Confrontation in the worst way. As she grew more beautiful and mature, it became more important for her to leave Confrontation. Her life there was stifling. Her brother was a violent man. He would punish her for the least infraction—if she dropped an egg, or overlooked a patch of dust when she was cleaning, if she burned the dinner beans or didn't get a stain out of his shirts or didn't bring him a beer fast enough. He thought he owned her because he was supporting the family. It was an abusive relationship, but without the sex. When he wanted a woman for that, he would leave Confrontation, satisfy his needs, and, days or months later, return. There were always rumors, all kinds of rumors, about missing women in the next town, but Bunnell was clever and connected. He was never charged. He was the law around there."

"How can you be sure he never—"

"Because Necey confided in me. She was a virgin when she met Moss. She had to hide her feelings because she was sure if Bunnell found out, he'd make her pay and make Moss pay, too. And it wasn't in her nature to lie to anyone, so it tore her up inside. But I think she experienced love and joy for the first time in her young life when she met Moss. It wasn't that she wanted to leave with the first man she saw, just to get away. They were truly in love.

"So I covered for them. Moss was boarding at our house, and I left Necey and Moss alone. I was supposedly chaperoning, but my husband and I took every excuse to leave the cabin and let them pursue a relationship. When Bunnell came sniffing around, I put him off the track, told him I hadn't seen his sister. But he was like a bull in heat. If he had known Moss was pursuing his sister, he would have snapped. And finally, in the end, when he found out, he did just that. I think one of your aunts finally told him. He must have smacked the truth out of her."

Alec crossed his arms and frowned. "Go on."

"When she told Moss she was expecting a baby, that man was over the moon. He insisted that your grandfather and I drive him to the next town to a jewelry store so he could get a proper ring for Necey. He took his time picking out just the right ring, a ring he thought Necey would love, and she did. She was twirling around the cabin when he put that ring on her finger the night we got home from the store. They had their whole future mapped out. They were going to travel, see Italy, perhaps settle there while Moss painted lofty architectural views. He was eager to branch out and stretch his talent to new heights. Necey had hardly been out of Confrontation except to attend church functions, and even then she was well chaperoned. Meeting Moss represented a new level of freedom for Necey in her unnaturally sheltered life. They were deliriously happy. They were such a lovely couple."

Katherine twisted her hands. "On this particular morning, on their last morning together, they had it all planned. Necey's bags were packed and stored in my closet. She and Moss were going to leave Confrontation for good. He was truthful about his marriage, which wasn't much of a marriage at all. He was determined to get a divorce and marry your mother. It was around dawn. The cabin was peaceful. Your grandfather and I were asleep in our room, and Necey and Moss were in the second bedroom when we heard an incessant pounding on the door.

" 'Bernice Brady!' Bunnell bellowed. 'I know you're in there, you lying whore. Open up this door.' The racket was loud enough to wake everyone on the mountain. Bunnell kept screaming her name, and obscenities, and I thought he was going to break down the door, so I let him in. I wish I hadn't. I'll never forgive myself for giving him the opportunity…"

Katherine took a deep breath and continued. " 'Where is she?' he screamed. 'I know she's in here.'

"Your grandfather and I blocked the door of the second bedroom. 'You need to leave our house, or we'll call the police,' we told him. I think Bunnell laughed at that point. He knew we didn't have a phone, and he was friends with everyone in the police department. He knew he was untouchable. It was then I noticed the shotgun he was holding in one hand."

Katherine's hands flew to her throat as if she were reliving the incident. Amelia rested her hand on her grandmother's shoulder, mutely asking that she continue her story.

"Your grandfather tried to stop him, but Bunnell was out of control, like a raging bull. He was waving the shotgun around and threatening us. He swiped us out of the way like he was swatting a fly and opened the door to our guest room, where he found them. They were in bed, Necey in a frilly white nightgown and Moss in nothing but his boxers. They were trying to hide under the comforter. Like children do when they're convinced you can't see them, thinking somehow the bedspread would protect them. Against a loaded shotgun. Moss was a painter, a mild, quiet man. He'd probably never even seen a shotgun before. He didn't stand a chance against a man like Bunnell.

"Bunnell pulled off the bedcovers and hauled Necey to her feet, almost wrenching her arm out of its socket. Moss tried to protect her, but Bunnell was a lot stronger than Moss, and he yanked him out of bed and dragged them both into the living room.

"Seeing Moss in his undershorts and Necey in a flimsy robe further enraged him. And he knew…you could tell he knew about the baby.

" 'How long, Necey?' Bunnell demanded. 'How long have you been whoring yourself out? And for what? A man who plays with paints?'

" 'Moss is a great artist,' Necey protested. 'I love him. We're going to be married. You see, he gave me this promise ring.' Necey held out her hand and flashed the fancy emerald-and-diamond ring.

" 'Is that what he told you? Did he also tell you he was already married? I did some checking.'

" 'He did,' Necey acknowledged. 'But he's going to get a divorce so we can be together.'

"At that point Bunnell grunted and ran up and down the cabin, waving his shotgun, a giant presence that cast a pall over the room. He stuck his head into the second bedroom, then went into our bedroom, rummaged through our closet, and came out with Necey's luggage. A pitiful two pieces, taped together. Her whole life was in those suitcases."

" 'You were going to run away without telling me or Pa? Did your sisters know? Of course they did. You tell your sisters everything. You three are as thick as thieves. Does everybody in Confrontation know how you made me look like a fool?'

"Necey came out from behind Moss and faced her brother.

" 'Bunnell, this isn't about you,' she said. 'This is my life, and I want to be with Moss.'

" 'You don't know what you want. Did he force himself on you? Did he violate you? And you just a child? He's making false promises. Don't yield to temptation. Sister, don't let him exploit your weakness. Fornication is the devil's work.'

"The only devil in the room that day was Bunnell Brady. And his evil, ugly side was exposed. He seemed to be warring with himself, trying to exert some control over his actions, but it was a losing battle.

" 'It wasn't like that,' Necey implored. 'We're in love. And I'm not a child. I'm a grown woman.'

"Bunnell choked out a laugh. 'You're too young to know anything about love. I thought you was pure, the last, best thing on this mountain, and I didn't touch you like I wanted to, but turns out you're nothing but a whore like the rest of them women. If you wanted a man, you could have had me. I loved you, Necey. Look what you done to us.'

"Necey was clutching Moss and crying, trying to reason with Bunnell. 'Bunnell, you know this isn't right. You're not right. If you really love me, you'll let me go. Let us go. I want to live my life.'

"At that, he slapped Necey across the face, swatted her with the force of a grizzly bear, snapping back her neck, stinging her cheek, causing more tears to stream from her eyes.

" 'Leave her alone,' Moss shouted. He was trying to be brave, but I could tell he was scared. 'I am going to marry her. I love her more than anything in this world.' He pushed Necey behind him again to shield her.

"Bunnell's voice was chilling when he addressed his sister. 'You git on home. Get out of my sight. You sicken me. I'm gonna think long and hard on your punishment. We're gonna pray on it together when I get back there.'

"Necey was defiant. 'I'm not leaving, not without Moss. I'm carrying his child.'

"Confirmation of his sister's pregnancy seemed to fill Bunnell with raw anguish and a mighty rage that hadn't worked itself out yet, and he reared up.

" 'I'm going to break both of his hands for touching you,' threatened Bunnell. 'He'll never paint again.'

" 'Bundy, no! I won't let you.' Necey screamed and pleaded.

" 'You won't let me?' echoed Bunnell. 'How are you going to stop me?'

"In what seemed like one motion, he grabbed Necey and flung her against the wall, raised up his shotgun, and put a bullet right between Moss's eyes. Bunnell was an excellent shot. I'd seen him shoot birds right out of the sky. Blood spurted out of Moss's head. Necey screamed and kept screaming and shouting his name. She ran over and held him so tight, but we could all tell he was gone. There was nothing anyone could do for him.

"Bunnell bent down to grab Necey's arm, and she reeled away from him.

" 'Get out! You're a monster! I never want to see you again. I hate you!'

"Bunnell scooped up the rifle, and he was so agitated he would surely have shot Necey if Will hadn't picked up a cast iron skillet and bashed him in the head, and he slid to the floor. Necey was moaning. I think she was in shock. I know I was. It was the worst day of my life. I tried to get Necey to move away from Moss, but she wouldn't let him go.

" 'He's gone,' I told her.

"Bunnell was starting to come around, and I think he began to regret what he'd done, or he was figuring a way to fix it, make things right again between him and Necey. But then he got up, the light of evil in his eyes, and stared at me and your grandfather. 'If you ever tell a living soul about what you seen here, ever, I will hunt you down and kill you and everyone in your family. I'm going to clean up this mess, and I don't want to see you Florida people around here ever again.'

"I pulled a sobbing Necey away from Moss,

wrapped her in my bathrobe, and your grandfather and I took her with us in our car. We drove down the mountain and parked our car and sat there until we could breathe again. We had our eye on the cabin, and several hours later, when Bunnell came out, we drove back up, gathered our things together, and packed up the car.

" 'You need to come with us,' I told Necey. 'Away from this place.'

" 'No, I got to stay. This is my home.' Necey was still in shock, but she was adamant. 'I can handle Bunnell. Now I have this over his head, he won't bother me. There's nothing he can do to me. I'm dead inside already. I deserve whatever's coming to me. It's my fault Moss is dead.'

" 'Necey, none of this is your fault. All you did is fall in love. It's the most natural thing in the world. Your brother needs to be arrested and put in prison for what he did.'

" 'Nothing will happen to Bunnell. Nothing ever does. He's killed before. He's even bragged about it. It makes no difference what he does. He thinks the Lord protects him.'

"I held Necey tight. 'Sweetheart, you're welcome to stay in this cabin as long as you like.' I wrote down my phone number and address in Fort Lauderdale and pressed it into her hand and told her, 'Call me if you ever need anything.'

" 'I want you to take Moss's paintings,' she said. 'He has dozens of them in the closet. Take them and keep them safe. I don't want Bunnell to get his hands on them. That's all I have left of Moss.'

" 'What about that one?' I asked her, nodding to

the painting of Necey in the living room.

" 'I'm going to keep that one.' Necey was defiant.

"I handed her the key to the cabin, saying, 'Don't go back home. Stay here and stay away from your brother.'

"Then she thanked us. That was the last time I saw her. The last time I saw our cabin. Of course we talked on the phone over the years, and she wrote me. But when I heard she had passed, that's when I sent Amelia up to sell the place. I thought Bunnell would be dead by now, or locked away behind bars."

"You can't kill a mean son-of-a-bitch like Uncle Bundy," Alec said.

"Do you know what happened to Moss's body?"

"No one knows. Bunnell removed it, wiped all traces from the cabin. Moss must be buried somewhere on the mountain, but Necey had no idea where. Bunnell never told her. As far as I know, they never spoke of it again."

"Alec, what are you going to do?" Amelia asked, her face etched with concern.

Alec rubbed his jaw. "Right now I want to go back to the hotel, have some dinner, and cancel our plane tickets. We need to drive these paintings home."

He turned to Katherine. "Thank you, ma'am, for telling me the story. I appreciate it. When Uncle Bundy is gone, I'd like you to come back up and see your cabin before we sell it. All these years, and you've never been back? I'm going to fix it. Somehow, I'm going to make it right. Find my father and give him a proper burial."

Katherine got up and hugged Alec. "Are you okay?"

Alec nodded. "It's a lot to take in, but I'm glad I know. It answers a lot of questions."

"Your mother raised a fine young man. She would be so proud of you. And so would your father."

Chapter Seventeen

"My grandmother likes you," said Amelia, as she and Alec sat on lounge chairs on the hotel balcony overlooking the ocean. The ocean was Amelia's go-to place. The comforting sound of the waves crashing onto the shore soothed her down to the roots of her soul. She could listen to that melodious sound forever. Being near the ocean refreshed her. It was her constant. The sky was midnight black, and all the stars were shining like diamond pinpricks in the heavens. She couldn't imagine living on the top of a mountain, landlocked, with no ocean, no lakes, no water for miles around. The forest provided another kind of peace, but it didn't even come close to the magnificence and appeal of the ocean. She was unashamedly a Florida person.

"I like her, too," Alec said. "I appreciate all the help she was to my mother. She knew both of my parents. She witnessed their love story. I feel a special connection to her."

"And now my dad wants to move her to Eternal Gardens. I mean, it sounds all shiny and great, and they call it independent living, but it's only one step up from assisted living, and then it's a straight shot to a nursing home."

"And she doesn't want to move?"

"No. Her life has been at her condo. She lived there with my grandfather. It's going to be strange for her to be all alone somewhere else, even though she'll be closer to my dad. He worries about her all the way out here. If she's closer to my parents, they could visit her more often."

"Have you seen the place?"

"No, but my dad says they have everything there, all in one building. Doctors and physical therapists come to you. They even take blood in your room. She'll get all her meals there. There are round-the-clock activities, a piano player, a pool, and a gym, even a library. Anything a senior could want."

"But it's not home. Is she going to go?"

"She doesn't see that she has a choice. I feel bad for her. I hear that once an elderly person moves, the change is often too much to handle, and they start a downward spiral."

"Could she move in with your father?"

"I think they'd kill each other the first day. You took care of your mother and lived with her for the last years of her life. How was that?"

"It wasn't easy. I was at work all day, so I had help from the relatives. That's why I don't feel I can leave Confrontation. Everyone pitched in and helped me care for my mother. I can't just desert them. And they helped raise me. I owe them a lot for that."

"If you could go off somewhere, live somewhere else, where would you go?"

Alec looked out at the ocean wistfully. "It is beautiful here. I can see why you love the ocean, but I wouldn't want to live any other place except Confrontation."

Amelia sighed. She sensed something big might be happening between them, but that was a deal breaker.

There was no way under heaven she was ever going to live in Confrontation. Whenever she pictured her life, it was here, near the ocean. Confrontation was out of her comfort zone in every way.

Alec took her hand, and she felt a definite spark, a warmth, a connection like they could tell each other anything, especially sitting in the dark, staring anonymously out at the ocean.

"I always thought there was something unnatural about the way I was conceived," Alec began. "You know, all those jokes people make about hill people. That somehow there was some truth to them. You've made them yourself."

Amelia bit her lip. "I'm sorry for saying those things. I was wrong."

"Whenever someone, a woman, got too close, I shied away because in the back of my mind I thought I was somehow less of a man or that I was tainted, you know what I mean? That I couldn't or shouldn't bring children into the world, with my background. That I'm not good enough."

Amelia's grip tightened. Her heart was breaking for Alec.

"I mean, I didn't think my mother had an ongoing relationship with her brother, but I did think that maybe one night something happened, that he snapped and forced himself on her, and that I was the unfortunate result of that unholy union. Whenever my uncle came around, my mother always made excuses to be somewhere else. She feared him. You could see it in her eyes. The fear and the loathing and the sorrow. And now I understand why."

"Oh, Alec," Amelia whispered, her voice hardly

audible under the sound of the relentless surf.

"But now that I know, I feel like I have the right to ask you to stay with me, to see where this thing between us goes." He gripped her hand tighter. "That is, if you feel it too."

Amelia broke contact and looked out at the ocean but continued their talk.

"Alec, there is something between us," Amelia admitted, but she had to be honest. "It's just that I can't see myself living in Confrontation or raising a family there." Maybe if she had met him in another place, almost any other place. She couldn't reconcile living the rest of her life there. Lovers isolated in paradise was one thing, but all she felt was stuck, in Confrontation.

Even in the shadows, Alec's face reflected defeat. "If you love someone enough, couldn't you live anywhere with them? Love conquers all, isn't that what they say? Isn't that the way it's supposed to work?"

She turned to him. Even love couldn't conquer Confrontation. "Could you ever see yourself living in South Florida?"

Alec shook his head. "I would never want to, with all the traffic congestion and the stifling heat. I need open space, cool, clean air. Room to breathe. I feel confined here in the city."

"Well, then, I'd say we're at an impasse."

Alec took her hand again, but this time he faced her. "Couldn't we just agree to disagree for tonight? Pretend we might have a future together?"

Amelia smiled. "I think I could do that." She desperately wanted to give it a try.

Alec pulled Amelia up with both hands, walked her back into the hotel room—he had splurged on a suite with an ocean view—and led her over to the bed.

He started undressing her. "Tonight, we're on neutral ground. We're not in Confrontation and we're not in Florida. We're just two people falling in love."

"Careful, counselor. You just used the L word." Amelia's heart was doing somersaults in anticipation.

"I'm aware of that," Alec said, touching her naked body, causing her to shiver in the air-conditioned room. Alec's body heat was warming her, and she was moist and ready for him. He managed to remove his clothes between drugging kisses as he levered himself above her.

"I love you, Amelia Rushing, weather issues and all," he chanted before he drove inside of her. She responded with equal need and passion.

Amelia was caught up in the moment, the "L" word on the tip of her tongue. And Alec was doing glorious things to her with his tongue, driving all coherent thoughts out of her head. It was more than just great sex, more than the fact that Alec was a great guy. Was it love? Or lust? Or both? All she remembered was screaming his name. She'd never done that before.

Making love with Alec was so much more than she'd ever imagined. And, she realized now, she was in love with him. How had it happened so suddenly? So completely?

Alec collapsed on top of her, and then he rolled off, but he never let her go. He wrapped his legs around her in a tight cocoon and fell asleep under the duvet cover.

She relaxed to the sound of his steady breathing, punctuated by the ebb and flow of the ocean, and she thought this room must be the most perfect place on the planet.

What's-His-Name wasn't a snuggler, she could remember thinking as she drifted off to sleep.

Chapter Eighteen

It was a sunny day. Blue skies covered Confrontation like a soft blanket, which put her in a positive mood. Not a rain cloud in sight. The air was cucumber crisp and daisy fresh. No humidity hovering like the oppressive heat in Miami. That's one thing she wouldn't miss about the city. She hadn't consulted her weather app once on the way back to Confrontation. She didn't need to. She had Alec.

Dragonflies were lazily diving. Birds were serenading from the surrounding trees. What was that song by The Carpenters, "Close to You"? Amelia was feeling lazy, too, relaxed, and satisfied, because she and Alec had just had delicious sex before breakfast and because she was near him. Those silly love songs weren't so silly after all. Everything seemed brighter and more in focus when you were in love. There was no help for it. She had fallen hopelessly in love with a hillbilly. The next thing she knew, she would be romanticizing Confrontation.

But what would it be like years from now, when the afterglow wore off, when she was haggard from hanging out the wash and cooking and cleaning with two or three "young'uns" hanging onto her tattered skirt hem? She could glorify it and pretend she was Daisy Mae Scragg and Alec was Li'l Abner. He certainly had the body for it. And she had explored every yummy inch of his 6-foot, 3-inch frame last night and again this morning. They had only been together a few times, but each time they learned more about each other—bodies and mind—and fell deeper in love. Each knew what the other wanted. Each knew the rhythm of the other. Alec was sexy as hell, and they couldn't keep their hands off each other. But one day she'd wake up from her post-coital haze and realize she was a worn-out mountain woman, more like Ma Kettle than Elly May Clampett. And then she'd have regrets.

Their ride back to North Carolina had been smooth and uneventful. They had talked and laughed the entire way like they'd been friends and lovers for life. They shared meals and found they had a lot in common. Spending all that time in the car only cemented their relationship. And they couldn't wait to get back to the cabin to stretch their tired muscles and make love. Amelia didn't remember ever being this happy, not with her former fiancé, not with anyone.

Alec checked his email as they sat side by side in companionable silence, daydreaming in their matching Adirondack chairs on the front porch of the cabin. Alec broke the reverie.

"We've got some nibbles on the property. We should probably follow up." His melodic voice signaled, "I really don't want to do anything about this, but—"

"Hmmm," Amelia murmured in protest, rubbing his arm. "I'd rather nibble on your ear. Right now? It's so peaceful. I don't ever want to leave this spot."

"I'm talking to Amelia Rushing the Realtor right now, not that hot woman I had in my bed this morning. Do you or do you not want to sell this property, young lady?"

Amelia shrugged. "Frankly, I don't really care. Oh, Alec, isn't it wonderful?"

"What?"

"Just being here together, doing nothing."

Alec smiled broadly and teased, "Even if we are in Confrontation?"

"Yes," Amelia admitted. "This town is growing on me." Confrontation was beginning to take on a well-worn patina like the glow on her grandmother's silver pattern.

"Do you want to take this conversation back into the bedroom?" Alec suggested with a twinkle in his eye.

"You're sweet, Alec Brady," she said, getting up from her chair and straddling him, "but I think we already had that conversation, last night and again this morning."

"True, but I never get tired of talking to you."

Alec pulled up Amelia's sheer T-shirt and bra, and moistened each of her nipples with his tongue. "Or we can just talk out here." He kissed her, unbuttoned her jeans, and moved his hand inside her panties. She moaned.

"Do you like that, Miss Rushing?"

"I love it when you talk like a lawyer," Amelia said, responding to his caresses and placing her hand on his growing erection.

"I think Alec Junior wants to come out to play," she teased.

"Alec *Senior*," he protested, feigning offense.

She hugged him, breathed in his woodsy scent that had become so familiar, and smiled, overflowing with desire.

Without warning, thick storm clouds moved across the sun and the sky darkened. Rolling thunder rumbled through the mountains, threatening a thunderstorm.

Amelia's body stiffened and she removed her hands from inside Alec's pants, pushed Alec's hands away, pulled up her jeans, and pulled down her T-shirt. Fat raindrops began to plop on the porch, dampening her mood, immobilizing her.

"Do you see that?" Amelia looked up. Her stomach tightened. She clenched her teeth.

"What," Alec answered, lazily following her gaze.

"I don't like the look of those clouds. I'm going inside before the sky opens up."

"Amelia," Alec cautioned calmly, "it's hardly raining at all, and even if it pours, we're under the overhang. The rain can't touch you. And it can't hurt you. You know that, don't you?"

Breathing heavily, Amelia clutched at her neck. "I hear thunder, and that means lightning. And we're surrounded by trees. My weather app didn't predict this."

"How many times have you known a weatherman to make an accurate prediction?"

"What if a tree fell on the house?"

"Are you afraid the house will fall in on the Wicked Witch of the East?"

Amelia stood and pursed her lips. "Are you calling me a witch?"

"If the ruby slippers fit…"

"You're not taking this seriously. We need to go inside, right now. This is a bad omen."

Alec raised his eyes to the sky again. The clouds

had completely obliterated the sun and turned what had been a bright sunny morning into night. Alec shivered involuntarily.

"You might be right," he said. "We'd better get inside. I don't think I've ever seen anything like this sky before."

Suddenly, a tall figure stood at the steps up to the cabin entrance.

Alec looked up. "Uncle Bundy."

"Hey, boy. How've you been?" Bunnell's tone was easy, but Amelia detected an evil undertone that chilled her to the core.

Alec turned to Amelia and spoke in a voice that appeared calm but was more of a command. An intense voice she'd never heard Alec use.

"Go inside. Now."

Amelia froze as she came face to face with the infamous Bunnell Brady. He was as tall and broad as a giant, with a disheveled beard and overgrown hair. His clothes looked like they had been through a war and needed to go through a wash. Were those specs of blood on his jacket? Had he just carved up his latest victim? A rifle was slung over his shoulder. He made quite a picture. A picture of evil. Of every child's nightmare. The monster under the bed.

Amelia's feet stuck to the ground like they were encased in concrete, and she couldn't move her lips.

"This must be the pretty little lady I hear has laid claim to my nephew's heart." Amelia stared at the apparition. Bunnell's voice remained benign, but she felt his evil slithering around her.

"I don't bite," Bunnell said, exhibiting a modicum of false charm. "Aren't you going to introduce us,

Alec?"

"She's not important," Alec said. "Go on, get inside," he instructed Amelia without mentioning her by name. When she didn't respond, he started to sweep her inside.

"She a mute?" Uncle Bundy asked.

"She's nobody."

Amelia's first instinct was to be hurt, but she knew Alec was only trying to protect her. If Bundy got wind of who she was, who she was related to, and how much she meant to him, there would be trouble.

Alec pushed her inside and closed the door after her. "Lock up."

"Don't worry. I ain't planning to poach on your territory."

"What are you doing with a gun?" Alec asked warily, sniffing his uncle's breath. "You've been drinking."

"Just gone huntin'," Bunnell answered. "Shot me a bear. Got him in the truck. I had some of the boys help me haul him in."

Alec expelled a breath and declared, "We need to talk."

"Heard you was lookin' for me, boy. What's got your nose out of joint?"

"Sit down."

Uncle Bundy grinned and placed his rifle against the door. He took a seat next to his nephew.

"This about your mama?" Bundy wanted to know.

"No, it's about my daddy," Alec announced.

Bundy's eyes bulged. "Your daddy? Now where did that come from?"

"I think you know what I mean."

Bundy scratched his head as if he were perplexed.

"I don't rightly know what you're talking about, son."

"That's just it. I'm not your son, am I?"

"Who told you that?"

"I know everything, so don't bother denying it."

Bundy grinned, baring his crooked teeth. "Exactly what is it you think you know that you're so all-fired-up to tell me?"

"I know my father was Moss Hathaway, and I know that you killed him."

Bundy tried to hide his surprise, but his nervous tick betrayed him. "Am I supposed to know who this Moss Hathaway fellow is?"

Alec speared his uncle with a steely gaze.

"You know exactly who he is. You killed him thirty years ago, right here in this cabin."

Bundy chewed on his inner cheek.

"And who told you this?" His smile was fading, and his voice rose an octave.

"That's not important."

"Could it be your new girlfriend who's snooping around, stirring up trouble?"

"Don't believe everything you hear."

"Marie Antoinette told me she's one of them Florida people. I ain't got no use for them Florida people. They's trouble. Always have been."

"Leave her out of this."

"I ain't saying I did nothing, but wouldn't the statue of limitations run out on a crime that may or may not have taken place thirty years ago?"

"That's *statute* of limitations."

"That's what I said."

"If the crime is a felony, there is no limit. There is no statute of limitations for murder."

Uncle Bundy pulled at his beard.

"I want to know where my father is buried," Alec demanded.

"I raised you, boy. I'm as close to a father as you'll ever get. Why do you think he's your father?"

"Are you denying you did it?"

"I ain't confessin' to anything."

"How many murders have you committed?"

"Murders? That's my business."

"Well, I'm making it my business. If you don't tell me where my father is buried, I'm going to the police and have you locked away."

Bundy reached back and with an easy motion, picked up his shotgun.

"I don't think you want to do that," Bunnell warned.

"I'm not afraid of you. I'm not my mother."

"I loved your mother," Bundy objected. "She was the best thing that ever lived in this world."

"If you call it love to murder the only man she ever cared for, in cold blood right before her eyes, then I don't think you know the meaning of the word. Your little reign of terror is over, Bunnell."

Thunder rumbled overhead, and the mountains disappeared in the darkness.

"Bad storm coming," Uncle Bundy predicted, pointing the shotgun at Alec. "We'd better get in out of the rain." He stepped toward the cabin.

Slivers of lightning descended and struck a nearby tree. A torrent of rain was unleashed from the clouds.

"Lightning's close. I ain't never seen it rain this

hard in as long as I can remember."

Alec imagined Amelia cowering inside the cabin, probably trembling under the covers in bed. There was no way he was going to allow Bundy into his house—well, Amelia's grandmother's house. She was terrified of rain, but deathly afraid of lightning. She should be more afraid of Uncle Bundy.

"Alec, let's talk this over. Whatever you think happened, it happened more than thirty years ago. It has nothing to do with today. Or you and me. I raised you like you was my own son."

"You left me to grow up without a father, and you broke my mother's heart. And now you're finally going to pay for your crimes."

"What's to stop me from shootin' you like I shot that painter fellow?"

Alec exhaled. Finally, a confession.

"Why did you do it?" Alec asked evenly.

Now the words flowed from Bunnell's mouth. "He was molesting your mother. I seen them in bed together. He was a married man and a fornicator, and your mother was an innocent virgin. And you shoulda seen them nasty pictures he painted of her in the nude. No court in the world would convict me. I was protecting my sister's honor."

"The way I heard it, they were in love and were going to run off and get married."

"Necey was mine. No man was good enough for her. Especially not that artist."

"So you decided to shoot a defenseless man between the eyes because you coveted your own sister. That's sick and disgusting."

Alec noticed the startled look on Bundy's face.

"I know who that girl of yours is. She's the granddaughter of that busybody Katherine Rushing. I know everything that goes on in this town. You think no one told me she was trying to sell our land? I warned that lady if she crossed me I'd kill her and everyone in her family. Now get out of here. I'm going to have a private talk with your girlfriend."

Alec reached for the shotgun, and Bundy knocked him in the head with the butt of the rifle. Alec fell out of the chair but refused to be cowed. He rocketed up, rubbing the bump on his head.

"I am not gonna hurt her none. Just play with her enough to scare her." Bundy started cackling.

"Like you did with my mother? If you touch her, I'll kill you."

"With what, your bare hands?"

Lightning cracked and struck another tree. The flash illuminated Bundy's weathered face. The wind was rapidly picking up speed, and Alec had to hold on to the porch rail to keep from being swept away. At one point Bundy lost his balance and almost fell backwards.

"It's up to you," Bundy yelled, trying to make himself heard over the howling wind. "I can't have you going to the police."

"I'm not going to go to the police," Alec shouted. "You are going to turn yourself in, take responsibility for what you've done."

"No one is going to the police. Here's what's going to happen. I'm going to have to take your girlfriend for insurance. If you don't talk, nothing will happen to her. If you do, then you know what I'm capable of." Bundy licked his lips. "I have not had me a woman in a long time. And from the looks of things, you got her all hot and ready for me. She's a pretty little thing, nice and curvy, just like I like 'em. But I hear she's uppity. Thinks she's too good for our town. I aim to teach her a lesson. I'm looking forward to taming her. She'll be learnt to mind when I get through with her. You'll thank me for it later."

Bundy turned and headed for the cabin. Alec prayed that Amelia had locked the front door and bolted herself into the bathroom or the bedroom. He also knew that Bundy had the strength to kick down any of the doors.

"Bundy," he screamed, his voice hardly audible in the torrent of rain and what felt like hurricane-force winds. Alec reached for Bundy and grabbed him by the back of his shirt. Bundy turned and belted Alec with his fist, knocking him to the ground. Soaked to the bone, Alec crawled across the deck and hung onto Bundy's leg to keep him from entering the cabin. He couldn't let anything happen to Amelia. He would protect her with his life.

Thunderbolts of lightning landed all around them, zapping trees and sizzling an overhead power line. Zeus was on the rampage. Odds were one of them was going to get struck. For some reason, Amelia's silly statistics about lightning strikes came to mind. They were playing Russian roulette with their lives out in this weather. Tempting fate.

Amelia was right. Sometimes nature was ferocious and should be feared. When he looked up, Bundy was backing out of the door.

"Drop your gun and put your hands up in the air where I can see them." The voice sounded like Amelia's, but she'd never be caught dead out in this storm.

"Amelia, what are you doing? Get back in the house and lock the door. There's a dangerous storm raging." *Not to mention a raging maniac on our front porch.*

Lightning flashed, and Amelia's face was white as a ghost. He could almost hear her heart beating and see her body shaking. He could hear the fear in her voice, but she held the shotgun steady. His shotgun. The gun in the living room. The loaded shotgun. The shotgun that had killed his father.

"I said drop the shotgun." Amelia's voice was authoritative as she moved out of the cabin. Bundy took another step backwards.

The rain was drenching her, and lightning bolts were flying, but she remained focused like an Amazon warrior. She had never seen lightning strike so close.

Bundy issued a challenge. "I'll bet you don't know how to use that shotgun."

"Do you want to take that chance?"

Bundy calculated his next move.

"You want to know where Moss Hathaway is buried? I'll tell you if you put down the shotgun."

"You first."

Bundy held the gun high in the air with both hands, suspended over his head as if he were contemplating dropping it. She wasn't falling for it. If she let her guard down, he would pull it down with one practiced move and use it. She wasn't sure she had the nerve to fire her weapon.

Hail pelted all three of them, but Amelia managed to stay upright.

The next instant, lightning struck Bundy's raised

shotgun and his hair stood on end. He shook like he was being electrocuted, which he was. His brain short-circuited and his body danced like a marionette and then collapsed.

Amelia screamed and threw down Alec's shotgun. The hand of God had surely struck Bunnell Brady down in a decisive cloud-to-ground strike that could have been packing anywhere from 100 million to one billion volts. And, true to form, the lightning strike had occurred at the beginning of the storm. Most lightning strikes occur either at the beginning or the end of a storm, she knew.

Alec seemed to be in shock. Uncle Bundy was a monster, but he had been a surrogate father to Alec all his life.

Amelia went to Alec and tried to soothe him. "What an awful way to die. Did you know that twenty percent of all lightning victims die from the strike?" She doubted that reciting statistics would be of much comfort to Alec at this point, but quoting statistics served to bolster her strength.

"We'll have to call the police," Alec said. "Now we'll never find my father. Bradys are legendary for carrying secrets to the grave. This secret died with Uncle Bundy."

Alec put his arm around Amelia. "Are you okay? You're shaking. Come on inside, and we'll get you warm, find you a blanket, take off those wet clothes. What possessed you to come out in this lightning storm? You could have been killed. I could tell you were deathly afraid."

"I was more afraid of losing you," Amelia said and fell into Alec's arms.

Chapter Nineteen

Amelia and Alec stood hand in hand over a freshly marked grave in the family cemetery minutes after the funeral service. A steady rain was keeping the temperature cool. Alec held an umbrella over Amelia's head, but she didn't seem to mind the rain anymore. In fact, she welcomed it.

The newly carved stone read *Here Lies Moss Hathaway, Artist, Lover, Father*. Aunt Barbara and Aunt Brenna stood back a polite distance.

In the weeks that had passed since Uncle Bundy's grisly death, a lot of questions had been answered. Once he was no longer a threat, the police opened an investigation and found eight bodies buried in unmarked graves right in the family cemetery. The record rainstorm had unearthed three of them, skeletons of women, including Aunt Shelley—Marie Antoinette's mother—and two other young women who had gone missing from surrounding towns. They solved a number of cold cases, bodies of people who had crossed Bundy over the years, for various reasons. But they didn't find the body of Moss Hathaway because it was already buried in the grave next to Necey's.

"He was a mean old coot, but he was still our brother," announced Aunt Brenna to Alec when he called on her after Bundy's untimely death. "He wasn't right in the mind."

Aunt Brenna and Aunt Barbara told Alec that, after a year of anger and pain and the cold treatment, their sister had finally agreed to forgive Bundy, but as a condition of her forgiveness he had to tell her where Moss was buried and, as a further condition, he must dig him up and bury him in a grave next to her plot, where he should rightly have lain. Bunnell would have done anything for Necey's forgiveness. And, in the end, he did what she asked.

"That way, when she died, she'd be at peace because she and Moss would be together through eternity," explained Aunt Barbara. "No one need know where the body was buried or who was buried in the next unmarked plot. But Necey tended her lover's grave every day until she could no longer make the trip up the mountain. She told us about the deal she'd made with Bunnell but made us promise not to say a word, for fear he might take retribution on Alec or on Katherine Rushing."

When Alec told the police about Moss Hathaway's murder, he also requested a DNA test to verify that it was Moss buried in the grave next to his mother's and that Moss was his biological father. After weeks of anxious waiting, the results were in. The test had proven Moss's identity and his paternity.

"Go ahead, Alec, and say a few words over your father," Aunt Barbara urged.

With tears streaming down his face, Alec whispered, "Daddy, I wish I had known you. I wish you had known me. I wish you could have met Amelia." He squeezed Amelia's hand. "Thank you for making my mother so happy, even for a short time. Rest in peace."

Amelia wiped her eyes with her free hand.

"That was beautiful, Alec," she said softly. "Now that he's had a proper burial, they're truly together."

Alec and Amelia said goodbye to Alec's aunts and walked hand in hand down the mountain.

Amelia fixed Alec a glass of lemonade and took some of Alec's homemade cookies on a paper plate and brought them out to him on the front porch. The rain was steady, but Amelia's breathing was even. She found the rain calming. It wasn't the ocean, but it was water, nonetheless.

As they ate cookies and drank in the nature around them, Amelia broached a subject she knew was on Alec's mind.

"Now I think it's time to tell the world about Moss Hathaway."

"What do you mean? The police know, the reporters have been swarming around asking questions. Everyone knows."

"But they don't know about his hidden paintings. Your paintings, now that there's no doubt he was your father. He has no surviving relatives. Everything he had goes to you."

Alec took a sip of lemonade. "I don't know, Amelia. I don't know what he would have wanted me to do. From what your grandmother said, he was a private person. He wouldn't have wanted a fuss made over his memory."

"Alec, he was an artist, a world-famous artist. I've been thinking. We haven't sold the cabin. I mean, I know we've had offers, but what if we turned the cabin into a museum, if only temporarily, so people could view his new paintings before they're scattered around the world. It would be a tribute to your father and your

185

mother."

"Amelia, your grandmother needs the money this sale can bring, to pay for her independent living facility."

"She has enough for now. We could keep the museum open for, say, a year and then sell the paintings before we sell the cabin."

"Where would we sell the paintings?"

"Honey, you know what a media furor finding your father has caused. Not only are there new paintings to be discovered for museums, personal collections, or institutions, but the fact that they've solved one of the biggest mysteries of the last century adds further cachet and will make the paintings more valuable in the collecting world. Any auction house would love to get control of this collection. Moss Hathaway's paintings will bring unprecedented prices because of who he is or was and because his life was cut so short, because they are beautifully executed in a completely original style, and because of the rarity of the paintings. Not to mention the remarkable love story surrounding the newly discovered works."

"You really think people would be interested in my father's paintings?"

"I guarantee it. And you can't just sit on these works of art. The world needs to see them. I have some contacts at the auction houses through some of my college professors and the internships I've had in the past. I know they would be interested. They'd use a concept like 'Rediscovering Moss Hathaway.' Or 'Moss Hathaway—Lost and Found.' They always say most paintings become available because of death, debts, or divorce."

"You've been giving this a lot of thought, haven't you?"

"Yes. I majored in art history in college, and I'd enjoy this a lot more than selling houses. Case in point, I can't even sell my grandmother's house. Down and out for the count after the first try. I've pretty much failed in the real estate department."

"You're not a failure. If you hadn't come to Confrontation to sell your grandmother's house, we never would have met. I think we were fated to meet."

"I think you're right," Amelia agreed.

"You can sell her house any time you want to. I didn't want you to at first, and I'll admit I might have been standing in your way. I like the idea of honoring my father. But if we refurbish the cabin into a museum, where would we live?"

Amelia's eyes flew open. "We?"

"You don't think I'm going to let you go back to Florida, do you, now that I've found you? You want to know when I first fell in love with you?"

"Tell me," Amelia said.

"I had pretty much resigned myself to spending the rest of my life alone, and then, out of the blue, this beautiful woman walks into my office. When I saw that run in your stocking, that did it for me."

"I snagged it on your poor excuse for a desk."

Alec chose to ignore that remark. "And then when I found out you were afraid of raindrops, well, that sealed the deal."

"So you were attracted to my phobias?"

"That and I knew this might be my last chance to find a woman I wasn't related to."

Amelia laughed. "How romantic. Tell me more."

"I realize we haven't known each other that long, but I've fallen in love with you, Amelia, and I would do anything to keep you here."

Amelia wavered. Of course she'd thought about staying with Alec. But how prudent would that be? What would she do for a living? If this museum project worked out, she could be a curator at this very small but important new museum. She could bring in some of Moss's earlier landscapes, display the love letters, do some additional research on the artist, and then wow the public with his portraits of Necey and scenes capturing small-town life in Confrontation. This unique museum might even put Confrontation on the map, import some culture. Of course there would have to be a museum shop, and maybe a new restaurant or two to support the new tourist population. Some vacation cabins. Her grandfather's dream of providing a place for his family to visit could finally come true. More outside people would see the benefits of mountain living, and she could sell property right here in town, if the properties weren't landlocked.

"Even if we didn't open the museum, when we sold the cabin, you would have to move out anyway."

"Yes, but if these paintings are worth as much as you say, I could afford to buy the cabin from your grandmother and build us another one nearby. I know the perfect homesite. We could custom design our dream home, with great views, right by the waterfall."

"There's a waterfall?"

"It's not an ocean, but—"

"There was a waterfall in one of your father's paintings. I thought he had imagined it. It looked like a scene from paradise."

"It is a gem. Not many people know about it. I'm sure my mother showed it to him on one of their painting excursions. There is a lot to love about Confrontation. And I think I can clinch the right-of-ways."

"That's interesting. My grandmother couldn't get them for all these years, and now that you'll be the owner, they'll just fall into your lap."

"Family is family. And if you say yes, you'll be part of my family."

"You haven't even asked me a question," Amelia observed, her excitement mounting.

Alec set his lemonade on the table and got down onto one knee to propose in the traditional manner.

"Amelia Rushing, will you marry me?"

He held out a ring. Amelia could hardly believe this was happening. She admired the ring. "Alec, it's beautiful. How did you have time to buy this? I've barely left your side since I arrived in Confrontation."

"This is the ring Moss Hathaway gave my mother when they planned to run off together. She always wore it, and when she died it came to me. I never understood its history before now. I had no idea who had given it to her. I thought maybe a jilted lover. I romanticized the whole thing in my mind, clinging to any theory except the one I was sure was no theory at all. That Bunnell Brady was really my father."

The square green stone sparkled in the sun and gleamed against a platinum setting. It was magnificent. She wanted to accept his proposal, but if she did, they would be making their home in Confrontation. A whistle stop, well, not even a whistle stop. Not even an official town. What kind of life could they ever hope to have here? What kind of a life would their children have?

But what kind of life could she ever hope to have if Alec were not a part of it? She couldn't live without him now. There was only one choice. She stopped all the negative thoughts swirling around in her head.

"Yes," Amelia said, jumping into his arms, sure of her decision. Alec hugged her and placed the ring on her finger.

"You won't regret it. My parents didn't have their chance, but our love story will have a happy ending," Alec promised.

Alec rubbed his chin hesitantly like he had something else on his mind. "Would you object if we added a room for Marie Antoinette?"

Amelia thought that would be a good idea, since Marie Antoinette didn't have a dad anymore, and she thought she could be a positive influence on the girl. The wolf was another story, but they were a package, so she'd have to learn to come to terms with Dr. Landrew.

"An instant family," Amelia reasoned. "I would like that."

"And there would have to be plenty of room for our other children when they come. My grandmother had nine kids. How do you feel about big families?"

Amelia paused to consider. "Do their names all have to begin with B?"

"No," Alec said. "You would have complete naming rights. Let's call your grandmother. I think we should bring her up here and let her live in the cabin until we make arrangements for the museum renovations."

"She would love that. She hasn't been up here for

thirty years."

"We can add on an extra room to our new house, if she'd like to live with us. We could make it handicap accessible."

"You would do that?"

"It sounds like she's having some doubts about moving into that independent living facility."

"I think my parents might object. They think they're doing the right thing for her and that once she gives it a chance she'll enjoy living in Eternal Gardens. They have services to support her, and she can socialize with people her own age and keep active instead of living alone in that condo with only her memories. And soon she won't even have those. I dread the day she no longer recognizes me."

Alec nodded, wrapped his arm around her shoulders, and hugged her. His eyes reflected sympathy and understanding. Of course. He had been through the same thing with his mother.

"It's rough when that happens. Let's at least bring her up here for a visit. Confrontation is lovely in the spring."

Amelia rolled her eyes and thought of the song "I Love Paris in the Springtime." Confrontation wasn't exactly Paris, but then, Paris didn't have Alec Brady.

A word about the author…

Marilyn Baron writes humorous coming-of-middle age women's fiction, historical romantic thrillers, suspense, and paranormal/fantasy. She's a corporate public relations consultant in Atlanta. She's a member of Romance Writers of America (RWA) and Georgia Romance Writers (GRW) and winner of the GRW 2009 Chapter Service Award and writing awards in single title, suspense romance, paranormal/fantasy, and novel with strong romantic elements. She's a member of the 2016 Roswell Reads Committee. She graduated from The University of Florida in Gainesville, Florida, with a Bachelor of Science in Journalism (Public Relations sequence) and a minor in Creative Writing. Born in Miami, Florida, Marilyn lives in Roswell, GA, with her husband, and they have two daughters.

Marilyn says: What's unique about my writing? I try to inject humor into everything I write. I like to laugh, and my readers do too. I tend to feature older heroines, because—let's face it—we're not getting any younger. I love to travel and often feature the destinations I've visited in my books. My favorite place to visit is Italy, because I studied in Florence for six months in my junior year of college.

Landlocked is Marilyn's tenth novel with The Wild Rose Press. To find out more about Marilyn's books, please visit her Web site at:

www.marilynbaron.com

Thank you for purchasing
this publication of The Wild Rose Press, Inc.

If you enjoyed the story, we would appreciate your
letting others know by leaving a review.

For other wonderful stories,
please visit our on-line bookstore at
www.thewildrosepress.com.

For questions or more information
contact us at
info@thewildrosepress.com.

The Wild Rose Press, Inc.
www.thewildrosepress.com

Stay current with The Wild Rose Press, Inc.

Like us on Facebook

https://www.facebook.com/TheWildRosePress

And Follow us on Twitter
https://twitter.com/WildRosePress